# THE YOUNG LANDLORDS

"If you are looking for a book that's hilarious, tender, original, and appealing to black young adults, then this is absolutely the one to choose. Paul Williams and his gang of the mostly inactive Action Group decide to complain to an absentee landlord about a particularly run-down neglected apartment building known as the Joint. Before they know exactly what has hit them they've bought it for a dollar and inherited a fortune's worth of bills, problem tenants, broken doorknobs, and a dozen other small plagues that with the aid of a sharp, sensitive, one-of-a-kind narrator, make a first rate, funny, wide-spirited novel."

—*Lone Star Book Review*

# THE YOUNG LANDLORDS

## WALTER DEAN MYERS

PUFFIN BOOKS

PUFFIN BOOKS
A member of Penguin Putnam Inc.,
375 Hudson Street, New York, New York 10014, U.S.A.
Penguin Books Ltd, 27 Wrights Lane, London W8 5TZ, England
Penguin Books Australia Ltd, Ringwood, Victoria, Australia
Penguin Books Canada Ltd, 10 Alcorn Avenue, Toronto, Ontario, Canada M4V 3B2
Penguin Books (N.Z.) Ltd, 182-190 Wairau Road, Auckland 10, New Zealand

Penguin Books Ltd, Registered Offices: Harmondsworth, Middlesex, England

First published in the United States of America by Viking Penguin,
a member of Penguin Putnam Inc., 1979
Published in Puffin Books, 1989
15  17  19  20  18  16

Excerpt from "When I Was One-and-Twenty" from *A Shropshire Lad*—
Authorized Edition—in *The Collected Poems of A. E. Housman*
is reprinted by permission of Henry Holt and Company, Inc.
Copyright 1939, 1940, © 1965 by Holt, Rinehart and Winston, Inc.
Copyright © 1967, 1968 by Robert E. Symons.

LIBRARY OF CONGRESS CATALOGING IN PUBLICATION DATA
Myers, Walter Dean, 1937–    The young landlords / Walter Dean Myers.    p.    cm.
Summary: Five devoted friends become landlords and try to make
their Harlem neighborhood a better place to live.
ISBN 0-14-034244-3
[1. Landlord and tenant—Fiction.   2. Harlem (New York, N.Y.)—
—Fiction.]   I. Title.   [PZ7.M992Yo  1989]     [Fic]—dc20   89-34036

Printed in the United States of America
by R.R. Donnelley & Sons, Harrisonburg, VA
Set in Times Roman

*For Augusta Baker*
*with thanks*

# THE YOUNG LANDLORDS

# CHAPTER 1

YOU EVER HAVE AN IDEA THAT REALLY SOUNDS GOOD UNTIL you do it and find out how stupid it was? If you ever need one, just hang around with me a little, because I got lots of them. I remember one time there was this big kid in my Current Events class who used to push everybody around. Well, I read in this book that when a bully—and that's what this guy was, a bully—did something like that, he did it because he thought nobody was going to fight him back. Bullies were really cowards deep down. That's what the book said. Anyway, I got the bright idea that I was going to show everybody how this bully, whose name was James Hall, was really a coward way down deep inside. So I walked up to him in the hallway and told him I was tired of him pushing everybody around. Then I told him that if he didn't quit right away I would have to punch him out myself.

He just stood there looking at me like I was a Martian or something. I figured the book was right. He was scared. A few kids in the class started gathering around, and somebody said there was going to be a fight.

"Ain't going to be no fight," I said, "because this guy ain't nothing but a turkey!"

Soon as he hit me I realized that the whole idea might have been wrong. When he hit me the second and third times I was *sure* it was wrong. Afterwards, when my friend Dean came over and asked me how come I started the fight, I couldn't think of an answer. Even if I could have, my lip was too swollen to talk. When I was leaving I heard another guy say, "Hey, see that guy with that busted-up lip and his hat on sideways? He's a strange dude."

I hadn't noticed that my hat was on sideways, but I wore it like that until my lip came down to normal. It's better being strange than just plain stupid.

But that was two years ago, and the Stratford Arms thing happened when I was older, and you would think I wouldn't jump into things so quick, right? Well, I still did once in a while. Nothing big, no busted lips or anything like that. But the Stratford Arms thing was almost as bad.

It all started up in Mount Morris Park at the Annual Numbers Runners' barbecue. Two years before, when they had started the State Lottery, the guys that ran the numbers racket started sending telegrams to the mayor's office about how they were being squeezed out of making a living. The mayor said that running numbers was illegal and that the lottery was legal. Anyway, the numbers people started doing things to make themselves look more respectable. One thing they did was to pay to have some abandoned buildings boarded up so that small kids wouldn't go into them and get hurt. Another thing they did was to start the Annual Numbers Runners' barbecue. A lot of people said that numbers were still wrong, mostly because it was illegal, and some people even said that a lot of the money went into dope. But still, just about everybody from the block came, and we always had a nice time. They had barbecued chicken, barbecued spareribs, charcoal-broiled hamburgers, potato salad, coleslaw, pies, cakes, just about anything you could think of to take on a picnic. The Captain, who was the fattest guy at the barbecue, was sitting at one of the tables just looking around and eating, which was his favorite pastime. He used to eat spareribs like he was playing a harmonica. He was fat, like I said, but he had little hands and little eyes. He would get a sparerib between his palms and then run it back and forth across his mouth, twisting it with his fingers as he did, and in about two seconds it would be clean. An ant would starve to death on what he left on one of those bones. Anyway, Gloria saw him sitting there and had to go open her mouth.

"Hey, Captain," she said, "how come you ain't out there running in the races? You might win first prize!"

Everybody thought this was funny except the Captain. They say he never smiled but twice a year. Once on his birthday and once on Christmas, and that last year he didn't even smile on Christmas.

"You all can keep that running stuff to yourself," he said.

His voice came from the middle of his belly. "You can't make no money running. You can't feed no family with it, either. Not 'less you running numbers or something 'long them lines.

"I don't understand about you young people anyway," the Captain went on. "You been to school and you don't know nothing, you got you a little bit of money and you ain't got nothing, got your whole life in front of you and you ain't going to nothing.

"What I do comes from not being able to do nothing better. What you do is 'cause you don't want to do better."

Then he made a big sucking noise on a chicken bone, looked at it to make sure everything was off it, and put it down while he was reaching for another one with the other hand.

"You young today," the Captain said, "and you don't do nothing for yourself. You worsen a chicken with his head wrenched off. You take a chicken and wrench off its head, and it run around and flop around and carry on. But it ain't got nothing to do but die 'cause it ain't got no head to use. Ain't that the truth?"

When he said that, everybody started nodding and going on and saying how it was true and all. Gloria didn't say anything, and I figured that was all there was to it. Even the next day, when some of the guys we hung out with were sitting in front of the park talking about the barbecue, we didn't talk about what the Captain had said. When Gloria got there she started talking about what the Captain had said, and then she said that was true and that running was nothing and we never did anything that amounted to anything. Well, that was cool, because every once in a while we talked like that. You know, Good-Doing conversations. We'd sit around and say things like, "Hey, life is rough," or "You got to work hard to get anywhere in this life." We'd talk like that for a while, and then we'd get back to the regular things we always talked about, like what was on television or what we were going to go downtown and buy when we got enough money to go downtown and buy something.

So Gloria went on about how we were throwing away our lives and how we had to start getting with it and stuff. Then she said she was going to start an action club. She asked if we wanted to belong to it, and we said, "Why not?" That was one of those ideas that I should have thought about. Gloria pulled out this piece of paper that she had typed up. On the top, in big letters, it said, "Action Group." Then, under Roman numerals, it had what we were supposed to be doing as an Action Group. Mostly stuff about doing things that had to be done and doing them right away. Then there was a place for our names. So we signed it. It was me, Gloria, Dean, Bubba, Omar, and Jeannie.

So far everything was cool. We had signed the paper and we could get on with being like we always were, right? Wrong! Gloria had another piece of paper with things that had to be done right away. On top of the list was World Peace. She thought we should write some letters to the leaders of the world and tell them what we thought about peace and stuff like that. Which was cool, too, but it was too hot to go upstairs and write, so we put World Peace off until the next day.

The next thing on the list was cleaning up the empty lot

near the corner. We put that off until the next day, too.

The third and last thing on her list was to do something about 356. That was a building on the same block that Gloria lived on. It looked like a real nightmare. If you wanted a real ghetto place you could pick that one. Funny thing about it, though, that if you stood about two blocks away and looked down the block where 356 was, it didn't look so bad. All of the buildings on the block were either dark brown or dark red, according to what they were made of, and looked about the same from a distance. But as you came closer you could see that some of the buildings were okay and some were terrible. It didn't take a lot to make a building terrible, either. All you had to do was to have a few windows broken out, some garbage out front, and enough graffiti on the walls.

The building at 356 had its share of garbage, graffiti, and grit, but it didn't have any windows broken out. Oh, yes, it was the only house on the block that had a name. It was called Stratford Arms. No one ever called it that, though. It was either just 356, the way the postman called it, or The Joint, the name we knew it by. None of the buildings on the block were really great looking. Most of them looked like old people still trying to hold themselves together. Maybe they didn't look great, but they were still trying. Some of the places, like 356, had given up completely. It was one of those places that had furnished apartments and gave out sheets and things. Some people called it a hotel, but it wasn't, because you had to live there by the month, the same as everywhere else. Gloria had gone over there and gotten the owner's name from the guy who handed out the sheets and

*8*

stuff in the renting office. She said he didn't want to give it to her at first, but she told him that she was tired of having the eyesore in the neighborhood where she lived, and he gave it to her, along with a telephone number.

So we went to the corner and called the number. The operator said that the number was not working. Then Gloria went back over to the guy who had given her the number, and he said he didn't know any other number. Gloria said she thought he was lying, and the guy just shrugged his shoulders.

We went down and sat on the stoop, and I was thinking that maybe we had better concentrate on World Peace. It seemed easier to get on the big things than the little ones. Then the laundry guy came. He was the one who brought the clean sheets and pillowcases to the place. We all knew him, too. We told him what had happened, and he said that the owner had three other places besides this one, and that the bills went to a place on 84th Street. So we got the number of the place on 84th Street, and the telephone, and Gloria called the place and asked for the owner. The owner's name was Harley, Joseph Harley, and he answered the phone himself. When he answered the phone, Gloria just asked if this was really him, and he said yes. Then she hung up. It was still only about one o'clock, and so we got the bus on Eighth Avenue and went down to 84th.

Writing a letter was cool, talking on the telephone was pretty cool, but just walking up to a guy and talking to him wasn't cool at all. We got all the way down there when Gloria started looking around and asking who was going to do the talking. Well, naturally, everybody thought she was, since it was her idea and all. Then she started in about how we were all in this thing together and she wouldn't feel we were really on her side unless we did some of the talking. Then Dean said that was okay, we would do some of the talking, but she had to start it. That seemed fair enough, so we went into this place and asked to see Mr. Harley. This place was the same kind of place that the one on 122nd Street was, only it was clean and nice. The place was called Goree Studios. The renting office had a switchboard, and there was a Spanish girl sitting at a desk typing. Mr. Harley looked older than my father but younger than my grandfather, which probably put him about fifty something.

"We live on 122nd Street," Gloria said after Mr. Harley had asked us what we wanted. "And we want to talk to you about that dirty, filthy place you got up there. Go on, Dean."

"Who? Me?" Dean is a tall, skinny guy, light-skinned and scared looking. When Gloria said, "Go on, Dean," he took about two steps back, and so did I. But then Omar, who hadn't been saying much, jumped up and started talking.

"Look, man," he said, "you are oppressing my people. You are making them live under conditions under which a dog should not live. And we are here to see that justice is done."

"You live in this building?" Mr. Harley said, turning red. "You live in this building?"

"No, we don't live there," Gloria said. One hand was on her hip, and she was beginning to point so we knew she was getting warmed up. "We wouldn't live in that pigpen. But just because we don't live there don't mean we can't speak on it."

"Yeah, we're the Action Group," Dean said. He had got behind Gloria somehow, but he could easily see over her shoulder. "And we came down here to get some action."

"So let me get this straight." Mr. Harley started to calm down. "You people don't live there, but you see you don't like this place and you want me to fix it up. That's right?"

We all yeahed him, and he sat there, nodding his head.

"What are you going to do?" Omar asked.

"Suppose I do nothing," Mr. Harley said. "What are you going to do?"

"A lot," Gloria said.

"Like what?" Mr. Harley asked. He was sitting back in his chair and looking like he had just won or something. "Like what are you going to do?"

"We'll come down here and picket this place, baby!"

That's what Jeannie said, and it sounded like a good idea, but Mr. Harley was still smiling.

"You got forty-eight hours to give us some action," Gloria said, "or we'll be down here with our picket signs. And you can smile all you want to, but we'll see who'll be smiling in the end."

"Who is the spokesman for your group?" Mr. Harley asked.

"We all are," Dean said.

"Well, suppose I want to contact one of you—how can I do it if you won't give me the name of your spokesman?" Mr. Harley took a pad from his desk and a pencil and looked at the group. "Well, who's the oldest?"

When I found out I was the oldest, I just about cried. I was fifteen and everybody else was fifteen, except for Jeannie, but I had been born in March and everybody else had either been born in the summer or the fall. That was a low blow. So I gave him my name and address, although I knew I didn't want to. But as soon as everybody else found out that I was the oldest, they jumped right on my case.

"Go on and give it to him," Omar said. "He can't do nothing."

"Now, sir, do you have a dollar?" Mr. Harley said to me.

"A dollar?"

"Surely, if you're really interested in the building and the improvements you're suggesting, you won't mind investing a dollar?"

I had a dollar and I gave it to him. He smiled and said that I would be hearing from him in a few days. Only he seemed really pleased, which made me uneasy.

The rest of the Action Group was all excited when we went over to Central Park West to get the bus back uptown. They were talking about what they had said and everything. I was thinking about one thing—he had my name and address.

"Suppose he sends out a hit man or something," I said.

"He ain't going to send out a hit man to get you, man, relax," Omar said.

"He could probably take care of you with a hit *boy*," Jeannie said.

"Remind me to laugh at that funny joke," I said.

"What we ought to do is to go down there and throw a

rock through his window," Omar said as we settled on the bus. "We must show the oppressor that we, the oppressed, can stick together and rise!"

"You're oppressing me with your breath," Jeannie said. "Why don't you rise and face the other way?"

"Sometimes violence is the only answer," Dean said.

"Shut up." I was getting mad. "Gloria starts this stupid group, Omar starts spouting his mouth off, you're talking about violence, and the only name they got is mine. It's a good thing Bubba didn't come. He probably would have called the cat a name or something."

They all cooled out a little, but I could see they were still excited. It was all right for them, but they hadn't given the guy their name and address. I told myself that I didn't have anything to be worried about. I really wasn't worried about a hit man or anything like that, but I was worried about him calling the cops and saying we did something to him or threatened him. I tried to think back on what we said to him, and I couldn't remember if somebody had said that we were going to get him or anything else that would seem like a threat.

That night I couldn't eat, and my mother asked me what was wrong, and I said nothing. Then my father asked me what was wrong. My father is one of these guys that no matter what he says he has to be right. Some of the time we get along, but a lot of the time we don't. The thing I hate most is when he's telling me what I'm thinking. That's one of his favorite little tricks.

"I know what you're thinking!" he says. "You want me to tell you what you're thinking?"

Then he'll tell me what he thinks I'm thinking, and when I say I wasn't thinking that he says I just won't admit it. Anyway, I wasn't about to tell him that I had gone down to this guy's office and sounded off at him and then given him my name and address. He'd probably go on about that until I was eighteen. So I told him I had bought a bag of French fries and ate them too fast. Then he went on for about an hour about that.

The next day they told Bubba, and Bubba wanted to go down and see the guy again and tell him that we had cut his time short from forty-eight hours to thirty-six.

"We do that, see, and we got the initiative," Bubba said. "We just sit around and wait, then he got the initiative. This is a war, see, and we got to act first."

"How old are you, Bubba?" I asked.

"You know I'm sixteen," he said. "Remember it rained on my birthday and my aunt gave me that money?"

"Good," I said. "Because I'm going to call that guy and give him your name instead of mine. You're the oldest."

"No, you can't do that, see." Bubba started licking his lips, which he always did when he was trying to think, which wasn't very often. "We got to let him know that we got a leader, see, which is you."

Naturally everybody hopped on that bandwagon. I didn't think a whole lot of the idea, anyway. He still would have my name, no matter if I gave him Bubba's or not.

We played a little ball, and then we just hung around for a while, and then I was going to go on upstairs. My father had come in my room last night and saw a crumpled-up McDonald's bag in the corner, and he had made a big thing about it. I remembered that I hadn't picked it up, and I knew he was going to find some reason to go into my room and see if I had picked it up. I was just about to go up when I saw Florencia, who I really liked a lot and who had taught me some Spanish.

"Guess who's going to jail," she said.

"Who?" Gloria asked.

My heart dropped right in the middle of my stomach.

"Chris."

"Chris?" Omar was surprised, as was everybody else. Chris was the last guy you would think about going to jail.

"Yeah," Florencia said. "They say he stole some stuff from that store he works in."

"The hi-fi store?"

"Uh-huh. They got another guy, too. You know that guy that hangs around Eddie's all the time?"

"Tall dude walk with a limp?"

"No, that dark guy that always tries to talk Spanish."

"With the doo-rag around his head."

"Yeah," Florencia said. "Him. He got a record and everything."

We sat around for a while longer and talked about it, but we found out that Florencia didn't know anything, and when we went around the block, we found out that nobody else knew anything either. Just that the store had been robbed about a week before and that they just broke the case. Dean got really upset because he and Chris were very close. I felt almost as sorry for Dean as I did for Chris. We sat on the stoop awhile, and then we saw Chris's mother come up to the house with his uncle. She was crying. They had come up in a cab and Chris wasn't with them, so we guessed he was in jail. His mother was crying so we didn't ask her any questions. And when Dean got up and walked away from the stoop, we all did.

"Me or your mother?" I was still thinking about Chris being arrested when I got home, and I couldn't figure out what my father was talking about. But that's another one of his little habits.

"I don't know what you're talking about," I said.

"I just wondered who you expected to pick up your garbage—me or your mother?" he said. He threw the McDonald's bag in front of me, and I bent over and picked it up. It probably meant, I figured, that I would have to hear his mouth for the rest of the night. I was right.

"You really feel that your mother is supposed to pick up your garbage, right?" he said.

"No, I don't," I said.

"You expect me to pick it up?"

"No, I don't," I said.

"You expect it to jump up off the floor when it gets tired of laying there and throw itself into the garbage?"

"No, I don't."

"Then how do you think it's going to get up off the floor?" he asked.

"I was going to pick it up later."

"Later? You mean there's a special time to pick up garbage from the place that you live? You're suppose to just wallow in your garbage until a certain time of day and then you pick it up and start living like a human being?"

16

"I'm sorry," I said.

"What are you sorry about?" he asked. "Sorry that it's time to pick up the garbage or sorry that you're the one that has to pick it up?"

I didn't say anything. If he could have heard what I was thinking, he probably would have started stuttering, the way he does sometimes when he really gets mad. Later, when I had finally escaped to my room, I figured out two things that annoyed me about my father. The first was that he was just plain annoying, and the second was that he wasn't annoying in a way that you could really jump on. If he hit me or drank a lot I could really get on that. But when he got on my case about picking up garbage, it was hard. I guess it's easier to take a person being a pain in the neck when they're wrong than it is them being a pain in the neck when they're right.

# CHAPTER
## 2

GLORIA CALLED ME THE FIRST THING IN THE MORNING. SHE said she was calling a general meeting of the Action Group, and we were all to meet at headquarters in a half hour. Now, let me tell you about Gloria. She was a little shorter than me, which is pretty tall for a girl, and not bad looking. She would have been plain looking except for her eyes. Her eyes weren't pretty, but they were odd. They looked just a little Oriental, which was nice and which suited her. Then she had a way of looking at you that made you feel self-conscious. At least it made me feel a little self-conscious.

Another thing about Gloria. She had this habit of saying things to make you ask a question. She would walk up to you and say something like, "Well, I guess it had to happen sometime." Then, naturally, you would say, "What had to happen sometime?" and then she would tell you what happened. So when she said for me to come down to "headquarters" I knew I had to ask where headquarters was.

"Oh, didn't I tell you?" she said, knowing darn well she hadn't told me. "I called Reverend Glover last night, and he said we could use that room near the gym for our headquarters."

Well, that was pretty good, because the gym was in a building owned by the church and it was always warm in the winter and cool in the summer. The room had a desk in it and a telephone, but I didn't remember the telephone ever working. I told Gloria okay, that I would meet her there in a half hour.

I thought my father had left for work already. He works for the Department of Social Services, but he hadn't.

"Good morning, sir," he said.

"Good morning," I answered.

"Would you care for the morning paper, sir?" he asked in this real sarcastic voice.

"No."

He finished his breakfast without saying anything else. Mom had made some eggs for me and I ate them. Mom didn't say anything either, so I knew they must have had a fight or something. Usually Mom takes my side if he gets on my case too much. When my father had finished his breakfast, he got his coat and then gave my mother this little make-believe kiss, as if his lips were going to break or something, and then left for work. I knew I was going to be late for Gloria's meeting, but I stayed around and helped Mom do the dishes before I left. I got all the way downstairs before I remembered that I hadn't made my bed. I went back upstairs and she was making it and I helped her finish. She said I was going to be the death of her yet. She was okay.

"This meeting is called to find out what we're going to do about Chris," Gloria said. "Because we all know he didn't steal any stereo equipment, and we all know that Willie Bobo is a thief and an ex-con so he probably did it all on his own."

"Then how come they got Chris?" Bubba said. He was eating from a bag of potato chips. Bubba was always eating, and he was so fat that he kept busting the seams from his pants legs. "If he didn't do nothing they wouldn't arrest him."

"My mother said they thought it was a inside job," Omar said. "Somebody let the crooks in. The window was busted out in the back, but it was busted out from the inside. So they figured maybe somebody had a key or something and then busted the window to make it look like a accident. And the only guy who had a key besides Mr. Reynolds was Chris."

"How about that other guy that works there?" Gloria asked.

"He don't have a key 'cause he drinks too much," Bubba said, emptying the crumbs out into his hand.

"I think he's guilty," Omar said.

"You got to be kidding," I said. "How long have we known Chris? He's not a thief, man."

"Why?" Omar asked.

"Why?"

"Yeah, why?"

"You ever see him steal anything before?"

"I never seen him hanging out with Willie Bobo before, either!" Omar said, as if he had won his point or something. "And when they got Willie Bobo with some of the stolen stuff, they asked him who let him in, and he didn't say nothing. Then they asked him if it was Chris and he said yeah it was! Don't tell me he ain't no thief! It's them quiet dudes that be going around ripping people off. You don't suspect nothing, so they can get away with it."

"I just never believed he would steal anything," Gloria said. "I just never seen him do anything wrong."

"Them the kind that be doing stuff like that," Omar came back.

"He went into the store with Willie or he was in there already?" Dean asked.

"He was in there already," Omar said. "Then Willie got a car and drove it near the side door. When nobody was looking, Chris opened the door and Willie come in and started taking stuff out to the car."

"You know, that's really weird," Gloria said. "I've known Chris ever since I was about five years old, and if you would have told me that he would steal something I just wouldn't believe it. I mean he's really a nice guy."

"Let me ask you something," Omar said. "You ever miss anything when you were around him?"

"In school I'd lose things but—"

"Yeah, you'd lose them all right," Omar said, "to him!"

"Who told you about it?" Jeannie asked.

"Who told me about what?" Omar said.

"About how it happened and everything?"

"That's the way it had to happen!" Omar said.

It turned out that nobody had told Omar anything, and he had made up the whole thing because that was the way he figured it must have happened. We were all pretty mad at him for doing that, in a way, but in another way we weren't. Because it made sense. Omar said that if we didn't believe it happened that way, tell us how it *did* happen. Of course nobody could tell how it did happen and nobody could come up with a better story than Omar. We thought Jeannie had something when she said maybe the other guy who worked there, a guy called Brownie, had stolen a set of keys and opened the door for Willie. But Omar had an answer for that, too.

"Now, you figure the police couldn't think of that, right?" he said. "They thought about it and figured out it wasn't true. They wouldn't arrest Chris for nothing. They got to have a good reason to arrest a kid."

All the pieces didn't fit together to make it sure or anything, but it certainly seemed that Chris was guilty. Anyway, we all said we would give him the benefit of the doubt, and Dean said he was innocent until he was proved guilty and that was the attitude we ought to take. Then we all said we would be his friend still if he got out on bail or anything. Omar went out to the Coke machine and got two Cokes for himself, and then he said that he would be his friend but he wouldn't hang around him too much in case Willie was going to try to bump him off and get rid of him as a witness.

"You can hang around him if you want," Omar said, "but

I don't want to end up in the newspaper as no innocent bystander."

That just about let the wind out of Gloria's sails about what we were going to do about Chris. She tried switching back to what we were going to do about picketing Mr. Harley, but the talk kept drifting back to Chris and the robbery. We probably would have sat around and talked about it all day, but Dean got us out of it by accusing Omar of really enjoying the fact that Chris was in trouble. And that really seemed what he was doing, too. He said he wasn't, but we still got on him, and it made things easier for all of us. Chris was a friend and, as far as we knew, a pretty nice guy. His father and mother were divorced, and he worked part time to help out. He wasn't the brightest guy in the world or the coolest, just a middle-of-the-road kind of guy who was pretty nice. He had been working since we knew him. In the winter he worked after school and in the summer he worked full time, as he had been this summer in Listening Land, a place where they sold record players, radios, some cameras and posters and things like that. We were all hoping—I'm not really sure about Omar, but the rest of us were hoping—that Chris wasn't really guilty, but it was hard to believe. Omar had said that the police don't arrest you for nothing. This wasn't enough by itself, but the fact that they had arrested Willie Bobo first and then Chris seemed pretty hard.

The next day was Friday and we heard that Chris was getting out on bail. His father and mother brought him home in a cab and took him upstairs. We hung around to see if he was going to come down, but just his father came down and left.

My father asked me about what had happened when I got home, and I expected to hear one of his lectures about how kids didn't appreciate anything they were getting these days and how hard he had had it when he was a boy. If I've heard that story once I've heard it a dozen times. I could even tell how he was going to twist it, depending on how he started out. And it was all going to lead to how he went to night school, worked hard at his studies, and got a job as a clerk for the Department of Social Services. But he fooled me this time. He didn't say anything. At first I thought it was because he had had a fight with Mom the day before, but he just looked sad. I hadn't told him much, just the things I knew for sure. When I saw he looked sad, I wanted to say something else, and so I said I didn't think Chris was guilty, and he looked at me and said he hoped not. And when he said it, he was twisting his ring around his finger, the way he did sometimes when he was upset about something, and I felt that he meant it with all his heart.

Now that got me a little ticked off. It really did. I just sat there and thought about my father feeling bad for Chris and all. The television was on and we were watching the news— something about the price of oil going up—but all the time I was thinking about Chris and the way my father seemed to be affected.

"How come," I said, getting my nerve up, "you yell at me for just having a paper bag on the floor and you get all upset about the fact that Chris might get in trouble?"

He looked at me and shrugged and then looked away toward the television. The news was just about over when he spoke again.

"Chris has a hard life at home," he said. "I just hope he didn't react to it in the wrong way."

I didn't even know that he knew anything about Chris. I remembered a year or so before he had gone to Chris's house to see if Chris could go on a neighborhood trip. My father was driving one of the buses and Chris was going to be one of the guys he was going to pick up. He wanted Chris to be monitor in the bus he drove, and I was going to be the monitor in the other bus. He had asked me a lot of questions about Chris that night and had seemed really interested when I told him that Chris's parents were divorced.

Saturday and Sunday went by pretty easily. Chris came down and we talked to him about everything in the world except the robbery. I caught myself trying to figure out if he looked guilty. Sometimes I know things, like people don't *look* guilty or not guilty. But still I look at them. Like you look at some guy's picture in the paper that they caught embezzling money, and you say to yourself, "Yeah, he's just the type."

Gloria said we were going to picket Mr. Harley Monday, but then we found out that Chris was going to some kind of hearing and so we waited around for that instead. When he came back we really felt great. For some reason we had thought we would probably never see him again. Then he told us that they just had some kind of preliminary hearing and that they were going to have a full hearing in two weeks and then set a trial date. He said he was going to have to get a lawyer.

The next day we were in the church office painting signs. Things like "Unfair" and "Who Needs Slums?" and "Slum-lords!" We had six signs in all. We had started out with nine, and we had really cool things to put on them, like "Roaches and Rats and Filth Really Hurt, Harley Takes the Money and Leaves Us the Dirt!" Which was made up by me. But we only got three lines on the poster before we ran out of room. The same thing happened to "Mr. Harley Unfair to Disadvantaged Minorities." The last sign that we messed up was because Bubba spelled tenant with two n's. We didn't want to look ignorant, just mad.

Anyway, we were in the church office painting the signs when Pat came by and said the mailman had just left a spe-cial-delivery letter in my mailbox. Naturally Gloria wanted us to take a break so we could all go over and see what it was. I told Gloria to mind her B-I business, but then she said it could be from Mr. Harley telling us what improvements he was going to make. I said yeah, but in the back of my mind I also knew it could be Mr. Harley telling me that he was suing me for threatening him or something.

So we all went over to my mailbox, guessing what it might be.

"Maybe it's something for your mother," Jeannie said. "When's the last time you had a special-delivery letter?"

"Never," I said, hoping it was for my mother.

Bubba said it could be from the school and maybe we all got one. His house was before mine and he stopped and

26

looked in his mailbox. He didn't have a key so he just looked in the slot but he didn't see anything. Then we got to my place and I opened the box. It was addressed to me! It was from somebody called Chasen & Diaz, Attorneys-at-Law. I felt slightly sick to my stomach. I opened the letter, which was jammed full of papers. They were all legal papers, and some of them had drawings on them. I took the papers upstairs and showed them to my mother. She didn't know what they were, and she called my father. He couldn't tell over the phone and told my mother to bring them right down to where he worked.

Most city buildings look terrible, and the madhouse my father worked in was no exception. The walls were a putrid green color except where the paint had chipped off and there was a putrid cream color showing through. There was a low wooden railing that separated the people who worked there from the people who came to get welfare. There was only one real office, and that was in the corner. Everything else was just desks. There were two desks, face to face, a few feet of space between them, and then two more desks. This continued along the wall until they reached the office. Altogether there were eight desks. My father's job is to check their papers when people are supposed to get emergency checks and to make sure the address and everything is right.

When we got down to his office, there was a fat lady sitting at his desk and he was looking at her papers. She was yelling at him and saying that he was a no-good Uncle Tom, and he just ignored her like she wasn't even there and kept looking over her papers. Then he told her something and she started yelling at him and looking through her pocketbook. Finally, after pulling out about three dirty handkerchiefs and a pack of old letters in a rubber band, she found what he needed and he stamped her papers. Then she smiled and started talking nice to him, but he didn't change his face one time. When she left, he called Mom and me over and took a look at the papers. One lady got mad because she thought that we were welfare people and were getting in front of her, but then my father told her that we were his family and we would only be a minute, so she calmed down.

My father said he didn't know what the papers were for either, and he took us into another office where there was a lawyer and showed the papers to him. He was a young guy, but he had a beard, which he kept pulling the whole time he looked at the papers. Then he looked up at where we were all standing around waiting for him to finish looking at the papers.

"Who's Paul Williams?" the lawyer asked.

"That's my son," my father said, putting his arm around me.

"Well, apparently he has just purchased a building at 356 West 122nd Street for one dollar."

My father looked at me and I looked at him, and then I told him what had happened with Mr. Harley and about me giving him the dollar and everything. Then my father asked the lawyer was it all legal.

"If you sign the papers they're all legal," the lawyer said. "It sounds like your son went down and complained to the owner about the condition of the building, and the owner is saying if you don't like the way I do it, do it yourself."

"But a whole building?"

"It's common for landlords to abandon buildings," the lawyer said. "What he's doing is abandoning this building by giving title to your son. Frankly, your boy doesn't have a thing to lose by accepting it."

Now, that's how I got to be a landlord. That's right, a real honest-to-goodness landlord. The lawyer had a friend of his look over the papers just to make sure, and everything was okay. The second lawyer that looked over the papers worked for the Legal Aid Society, and he said he would be my attorney, free of charge, if I decided to accept. My father said it was okay and I was in business. That is, me and the Action Group. I decided that we would all be landlords because that's how we got into it in the first place. The Legal Aid lawyer, Charlie Turner, drew up a lease form for us to have the tenants sign, saying that they accepted the terms we set forth, and we sent them out. Everybody signed them and sent them back to us, and I called a meeting of the Action Group to decide how we were going to fix up our building.

# CHAPTER
## 3

IT TOOK US A WEEK TO SETTLE DOWN AFTER WE DISCOVERED that we were now the owners of the building. When we first walked into the renting office on the first floor and closed the door behind us, we were all grinning like anything. Then we got serious.

"I think we should raise the rents," Omar said. "That way we can get the money to fix up the place."

"Our new lease says we can't raise the rent unless we do fix it up," I said. "It's a consumer-oriented contract. What that means is that we're not in it to make a lot of money but to run the place right."

"I think that Harley is a dirty character," Gloria said. "He's shifting all the responsibilities to us."

"The first thing we have to do," Dean said, "is to find out who we got living in the building and find out what kind of complaints they have."

That seemed like a good idea and so we called our first tenants' meeting. We were all going to meet in the lobby. Only on the day that the meeting was to be held nobody showed up in the lobby except the six of us. Then we found out that Dean, who was supposed to notify all the tenants of the meeting, had forgotten to do it. That's how come we decided to knock on people's doors. We thought it would be best if just some of us went around, and it was decided that me, Gloria, and Dean would be the ones.

We also found out that Florencia was going back to Puerto Rico to live with her grandmother. Scratch one of the Action Groupees.

The first place we went was down to the basement apartment where a guy named Petey Darden lived. Along with the papers that Mr. Harley had sent us was a letter explaining how Mr. Darden collected the garbage every day and kept the halls clean. In return for doing this he didn't have to pay any rent. Also, the letter said, sometimes he did light repairs in Mr. Harley's other houses, but he didn't do any in 356.

Mr. Darden was okay. He said he got a letter from Mr. Harley saying that we were the new owners, and he wanted to know if we wanted to have the same arrangement with him that Mr. Harley did, and we said yes. Mrs. Darden didn't say much but just kept looking at us like she thought we were going to change into something weird at any moment. None of us said too much to her. We all shook hands with Mr. Darden and then we went up to the first floor. The renting office is on the first floor and there are only two apartments on it. The rest of the floors have three.

The apartments are labeled A, B, and C. On the first floor the renting office is the A apartment. The B apartment was rented by a lady named Lula Jones.

"You who?"

"We're the new owners of the building," Gloria said. "And we're just coming around to meet all the tenants."

"Well, why you knocking on my door?" Mrs. Jones didn't open her door all the way. She had the chain on, and you could just see one eye peeping through the crack.

"We're the new owners of the building," Gloria said again. This time her eyebrows were going up and down, and she pronounced each word slowly and carefully. "And we are going around to meet all the tenants because we think the building should be a nice place to live, and if we all co-operate perhaps—"

That's all the far she got when Mrs. Jones slammed the door shut. We all looked at each other, and then Gloria put her ear to the door to see if she could hear anything. She couldn't, so we went on to the next apartment. According to the list we got from Mr. Harley, the C apartment was rented by a Mr. Gilfond. He wasn't home, and neither was his wife, so we went up to the second floor. We didn't say much to each other, but we were getting a few doubts, at least I was getting a few doubts. Just to be different we tried the C apartment first, which was rented to a Miss Robinson.

"Who you say you was?" Miss Robinson was small and

coffee-colored. She was wearing a housecoat that went all the way down to the floor.

"We're the new owners of the building," Dean said.

"When you going to do something about my stove?" Miss Robinson said.

"Your stove?"

"Yeah." Miss Robinson moved away from the door and held it open like we were supposed to come in, and so we did. "It ain't worked right since we moved into this raggedy place. You gonna fix it?"

"Well, yes, we are," Gloria said. "Now what apartment is this again?"

"Don't be taking my apartment number down," Miss Robinson said. "Every time that Harley come over here he be taking my apartment number down and don't fix nothing! You know what my apartment is, ain't that many apartments in this raggedy building!"

"That's why we're coming around, to see what's wrong so we can arrange to have it fixed," Gloria said.

"You ain't doing nothing," Miss Robinson said, "except taking down numbers, the same as that other dude!"

"What's going on?" Another woman came out of the bedroom. She was about the same size as Miss Robinson and looked a lot like her except she was a little darker.

"These the new landlords," Miss Robinson said.

"Ain't they some children?" the other woman said.

"Don't make no difference," Miss Robinson said. "All they doing is taking numbers the same way that other dude did. Look at this stove—"

She went over to the stove and turned on all four burners and only two came on. Gloria started writing that down, mostly because she didn't know what else to do, I guess, but Dean reached over and turned something. Then he turned on the gas, and the burners that didn't come on before came on.

"Who you?" Miss Robinson asked.

"Dean."

"You a landlord, too?"

"We all are," Dean said.

"Least you some good if the rest ain't. Maybe you people will be some good, I don't know."

"Now, you're Miss Robinson?" Gloria asked.

"I'm Tina and this is my sister, Johnnie Mae. We both Miss Robinson."

"How come you ain't nothing but some children?" Johnnie Mae asked. "I ain't never heard of no children landlords before."

We tried explaining a little about how we got to be the new owners of the building, but they didn't really seem to care. They asked us if we wanted anything to eat, and we said no. When we got out in the hall, me and Gloria both gave Dean five. That was our first success as landlords.

"How come you know about fixing stoves?" I asked Dean, wishing it had been me that knew.

"Well," said Dean, trying to look cool, "that valve was pointing to off, and when I see something that points to off and it don't work, I point it to on."

Nobody else was home on that floor, and Gloria made a note of that. By now I felt pretty good. At least somebody

34

liked us and we had got something to working. We were thinking that between all of us we could probably fix just about everything that was broken in the whole place if we had to.

"Then the things we can't fix we can get a handyman or something to come look at," Gloria said. "The thing we got to do is get things fixed right away. That way it won't get out of hand."

We all agreed to that and also talked about getting up a special repair fund. We hadn't met Askia Ben Kenobi yet. When Gloria saw the name on the list, she showed it to me and Dean, and we thought that maybe the guy was a foreigner or something. That was what he was . . . something.

"Do not speak until I have grasped the meaning of your aura!" Askia Ben Kenobi stood in the doorway with both hands in front of him. He was wearing a robe, like the kind you see in *National Geographic*, with a hood and everything. He stood there with his hands in front of him for a moment, and we stood in the hallway. We couldn't see into his apartment because it was almost dark except for some red light that came from behind the door. There was some incense burning and some music, which was as spooky as the red light and the incense.

"What is your business with Askia Ben Kenobi?" He bowed low, and this time he turned his palms up facing us. I looked at Gloria and then at Dean. Dean started laughing a little, and then he really cracked up. Quick as a shot this Askia Ben Kenobi straightened up. He stepped back into his apartment, and I thought he was going to shut the door, but instead he did a little turn and snatched his robe off. Zip! It was off and he was standing there in nothing but these little short pants. Then he screamed and went into a karate stance.

I hopped back about three steps and Gloria stepped on my foot as she went past me. Dean jumped a little but he was still laughing. Then this guy hops out into the hallway and does a karate chop in the direction of Dean, only he misses Dean and chops right through the banister! No lie. The guy chops right through the banister! I'm not the bravest guy in the world on a good day, and this wasn't a good day. I jumped down the whole flight of stairs, and Gloria was right with me. We hit the bottom of the landing in a heap. I got up first and looked up and saw Dean coming over the side of what was left of the landing because Ben Kenobi was chopping the rest of it up. *Wham! Wham!* Every time he swung, the wood would break up and pieces of the banister would come flying down. Dean hit the stairs and on his next jump landed right where Gloria was still trying to get up, and they went down again. By this time I was halfway together and started for the first floor and the safety of the street. Gloria got up again, and Dean, holding his leg, came behind her.

By the time we got to the first floor the police were there. I figured somebody must have heard the noise. I leaned against the wall, too out of breath to talk, and pointed upstairs.

"There they are! Them's the hoodlums!" It was Mrs. Jones, the lady who had slammed the door on us on the first floor. And it was us she was pointing to.

One cop grabbed me and spun me around and twisted my hand behind my back. Another one grabbed Dean, and before I knew what was happening, me and Dean were handcuffed together. I kept looking around for Askia Ben Kenobi, but he was gone.

"They the ones! They the ones!" Mrs. Jones was in the hallway, pointing at me and Dean and Gloria. She had her finger pointed right at us, about a inch from our faces and shouting to beat the band. Some people on the street came to the door, and I heard somebody saying that they got the guys who was robbing apartments.

Then some more cops came and they brought a girl with them and asked her if we were the ones that took her pocketbook, and she said that Dean wasn't one of them but I looked a little like one of the guys.

While me and Dean was getting ourselves handcuffed, Gloria was screaming about us being the landlords, except the cops didn't get it that way and they was talking about us being the Spanish Lords or something. A minute later the three of us were in a police car. Then guess who sticks his face in the window asking what we did? Bubba!

"What did y'all do?" he said, looking into the window.

"Nothing!" Dean yelled at him.

"You must have done something or they wouldn't have you in the police car," he said.

Yeah. Right. They got us down to the precinct, and lucky for us, we had the letter from Mr. Harley and told the desk captain what was going on. He didn't believe us, naturally, and told us that he was going to book us anyway. Then he called Mr. Harley, who he couldn't get, and then Gloria's father, who he did get. All in all we were down at the station for nearly three hours before we were released. We got a lift from Gloria's father and heard his mouth all the way home about what we should have done and what he would have done if the cops had tried to arrest him. He said he was thinking about suing, anyway.

When we got back to our place, it was almost midnight and my father was sitting on the stoop. He had his attitude on, wearing it like a straw hat or something. Then Mr. Wiggens, who is Gloria's father, started telling my father what had happened. I thought that would cool things out some, but when we got upstairs he started his act.

"Why didn't you call a lawyer?" he said.

"I don't know," I said.

"You don't know? You just give up your civil rights and you don't know why?"

He went on and on the way only he can do, and he made some sense for a change, only he thought it was cool just because he was right, and it wasn't, not as far as I was concerned, anyway. My mother came in when he had gone to bed and asked me if I wanted a sandwich, and I said okay. I had forgotten I hadn't eaten, and the sandwich was right on the money.

When I woke up the next morning, my knee was sore and my left wrist where I had been handcuffed to Dean. I was laying in bed trying to figure out if I had been a victim of police brutality when the doorbell rang and my mother came in and said that there was some white lady who wanted to see me. I didn't know who she was, but my mother said she was from some kind of city agency. I got dressed and went into the kitchen where she was sitting. She was thin, and had those kinds of glasses that are really just half a glass and people look over the tops a lot. Her hair was pushed back and tied behind her head. Everything she wore was either black or brown except for a button that said, "Long Live The Grateful Dead." The way her mouth was fixed it seemed that she was mad or something. She was, too. Mom didn't say anything about a guy being with her, but there was one. He was heavy and sloppy looking, with chewed-up fingernails and a stain on his suit jacket.

"I don't know if this is supposed to be a joke, Mrs. Williams," the woman said, "but if it is I don't consider it very funny."

Mom looked at her as if she were crazy. And then she looked at me and I shrugged, because I didn't know what she was talking about either.

"This is typical," the guy said. "You get a slumlord and then they get somebody else to take ownership of the building."

So that was what it was all about. I went and got the papers and told them the whole story, which I was now getting pretty tired of doing. They kept giving each other looks to see if the other one believed the story, and then finally the woman turns back to me and starts her mouthing off.

"Well, if you're the owner of the building—and I still have my doubts," she said, standing up, "then we're here to register our complaints to you. We're from the City Commissioner's office, and we received a complaint that there is no banister on the top floor. Do you realize what a safety hazard that is? Do you realize that there's an old lady up there who could fall and kill herself because you allowed that banister to get into the condition it's in?"

"We went up there to take a look," the guy said, "and what we saw is just criminal!"

I didn't believe my ears. Here a tenant karate chops the banister to little pieces, and then the very next morning somebody calls the Commissioner's office to complain about it.

"I'll get it fixed," I said. I wasn't about to explain anything more.

"When?" The woman said that with a voice so cold you could have used it to keep ice from melting. She held up a clipboard that she was going to write down my answer on.

"When I get good and ready," I said. "Now why don't you people just get out of here."

I don't know why I said that, really. I wasn't really mad at them or anything. But I was frustrated. Right, that's the word, frustrated. I didn't want to hear any of the things they had to say about the safety or about why I should have it fixed. I mean, I *knew* all those things and it didn't help a bit. Anyway, they left and said that I had sixty days in which to get the banister fixed or the city would have it done and collect rents to pay for it. Sixty days? Everybody in the building could go up there and fall off in sixty days! I was almost ready to say that, too, when I remembered I was the owner.

I called my so-called Action Group people together and told them what had happened. We came to an easy decision. We were going to have to tell Askia Ben Kenobi he had to move. I tried to be as casual as I could when I told Dean to go up that afternoon, after one o'clock, and tell the guy he had to move. It didn't quite work.

"No way, man," Dean said. "You must be out your mind. I wouldn't go up there and talk to that guy again if I could take your body for him to beat on. You see what he did to that banister? Can you imagine if he hit me?"

"Let's get Mr. Darden to tell him," Jeannie said.

I was really beginning to like Jeannie. I took her with me when we knocked on Mr. Darden's door. It all seemed simple enough. Mr. Darden goes and says how he hates to be the one to tell him and all but he had to move right away. Only Mr. Darden didn't like the idea any more than Dean had.

"Son, when you reach my age life is precious," Mr. Darden said. "You don't go around telling no crazy people they got to move. In fact, you don't go around telling crazy people they *got* to do anything. Now, if I go up there and tell that fellow he has to move and he jumps up and does bodily harm to me, who is going to take care of my wife? Who is going to feed my parakeet? Who is going to do all these things? You? No, my friend. What I suggest that you do is to get you an eviction notice form and give that to him by sliding it under his door when he is not around."

"That'll get him out?" I asked.

"No," Mr. Darden said. "Not as long as he pays his rent it won't. But it might make you feel better."

"Thanks."

"Any time, son, just call on me."

What Mr. Darden did do was to help me and Dean patch

up the banister. When we had finished, it was halfway together, but he said he really wouldn't trust it.

I was still determined to get Askia Ben Kenobi out of the house, and I went down to my father's office and spoke to that lawyer again. He said he had about as much chance of putting him out as I had. I told him that didn't make any sense because he didn't live there. He said I was beginning to get the picture.

# CHAPTER
# 4

"I DON'T KNOW EXACTLY WHAT HAPPENED," CHRIS SAID. "ALL I know is that one day I was sitting out on the stoop and these two guys come over and one stood and the other guy sat next to me. He asked me if I knew where he could buy any hi-fi equipment, and I told him he could come down to the store where I worked. Then he said he heard I could give him a special price."

"A special price?" Bubba repeated.

"Yeah, and he was talking like this—" Chris leaned back and started talking out of the side of his mouth. " 'I heard you could give me a special price.' As if it was all hush-hush and everything. Then I got scared, because the store had been robbed over the weekend, and I thought maybe these were the guys that did it or something. So I asked him who told him that, and then he said Willie Bobo and looked at me and winked."

"And what did you do?" I asked.

"At first I didn't do nothing." Chris said. "And then he winked again so I winked back."

"How come you winked back?" Gloria asked.

"I don't know," said Chris. "What do you do when a guy sits next to you and starts winking at you?"

"You don't be winking back," Gloria said.

"I never heard of nobody getting arrested for winking before," Chris said.

And he was right, too.

"Then what happened?"

"Well, I was real nervous by that time, and the guy was saying something about when could he see some stuff. And I said I didn't know—"

"Why you say all that stupid stuff?" Bubba asked. "Here you sitting there suppose to be innocent and everything, and you running down all that stupid stuff and winking and carrying on—"

"That stuff is only stupid when you guilty," Chris said. "What would you have said?"

"I'd a said, 'I don't know what you two guys are talking about,' and then I'd a said, 'If you don't leave immediately I'll call the police.'"

"They were the police," Chris said.

"Yeah, but they wasn't acting like the police, so when you said you was going to call the police they would have thought you was innocent because you wouldn't call the police if you was guilty, see? When you didn't call the police they knew you was guilty because they was talking about the robbery and you should have been nervous."

"I was nervous."

"Yeah, but you was nervous for the wrong reason," Bubba said. "That's why they arrested you."

"You'd make a good cop," I said to Bubba. "You think everybody is guilty of something."

"So go on with the story, Chris."

"That's about it. I said I didn't have anything to show them, and they ask me if Willie Bobo had it all, and I said I didn't know, and then they pulled out their badges and arrested me."

"Just like that?"

"Just like that."

"I don't think you're really guilty," Bubba said.

"Thanks a lot."

"Because if you was really guilty you wouldn't sound so guilty," Bubba said. "So either you're innocent and you sound guilty because you're innocent, or you're guilty and you're trying to sound guilty so everybody will think you're innocent. But I think you're innocent."

But what nobody could figure was why Willie Bobo said that Chris was in on the robbery if he wasn't. Gloria said we should hire a private detective to work on the case, and that sounded like a good idea, but when we called a few private detectives they told us that we'd have to pay a hundred dollars a day plus expenses. That was the end of that. Then Jeannie, who was beginning to look a lot smarter than I used to think she was, said that we could scout around and see

what information we could come up with in the neighborhood and then turn it over to the police. I don't know if that
seemed like a good idea because it was really good or because it was cheap. Somebody asked how you should go
about asking around, and we agreed to play it by ear, whatever that meant.

The first thing we found out was that not too many people
cared about any of it. People would say things like, 'Ain't it
a shame,' and things like that, but nobody seemed to really
care. There was a cop who used to hang out in the rib joint
all the time, and we asked him what he thought about it, and
he said that sometimes guys like Chris get into trouble because they think they're smarter than anybody else.

After a week had passed, I called a meeting of the Action
Group so that we could get a progress report. There wasn't
any progress. We didn't know anything more than we had
known to begin with. We also talked about hiring an accountant, and everyone was more or less for that. The main
reason that we were going to hire an accountant was because
the rent at Stratford Arms was due the next week. We
thought it would be better if we could tell everyone to send
the rent to our accountant. It would sound more official.

We were just about to break up the meeting when one of
the Robinson sisters, the light-skinned one, came by and
said that the water wasn't running in her toilet and that
Mr. Darden wasn't around to fix it. We said okay, and she
asked us if we would hurry up because she had to use the
bathroom. Then we got into a women's lib argument with
Gloria.

"I can fix a toilet just as well as you guys," she said. "So don't come off telling me about what's women's work and what's men's work!"

"You can't fix no toilet," Bubba said. "You probably just learning to use one right!"

"Bubba, you're so funny," Gloria said in this real sarcastic voice. "Remind me to write a memo to myself to laugh."

Anyway, what happened was that Gloria and Jeannie were going to go fix the toilet. I went along just to see them do it. They got a plunger, a pair of pliers, and a long wire with a crank on the end called a snake. (These were all down in the basement near where the furnace was, and we had seen them when we were down there before.) So we get them and go up to the Robinson sisters' place. Tina was on her way out and told us to make sure that we close the door when we left. I said okay and we went into her bathroom.

Now, the first thing you saw when you went into the bathroom was that it was pretty messy. That was to begin with. There were bobby pins and curlers and that kind of thing all over the sink, and there were dirty clothes in the bathtub. I figured she probably was going to take them to the laundry or something. Gloria had the snake and Jeannie had the other stuff. This was supposed to be strictly a female operation, and they wouldn't even let me carry anything.

Jeannie lifted the toilet seat and saw that it was almost full of water. The water looked kind of murky, too.

"Darn it!" Gloria said. "Sometimes if you pour some hot water down the toilet it unstops it. If you pour any more in this toilet it'll be all over the floor."

Jeannie agreed, and so they put the plunger into the toilet. They pushed it in carefully so that none of the water would spill out, and they jiggled it up and down but nothing happened. They did this for a while, and then Jeannie said that she didn't think it was going to work, so they started using the snake.

Well, the snake seemed pretty cool. You take this long piece of wire and you push it into the john, and then it pushes anything that's down there out of the way and the water goes down. Only instead of going around the bend, which is what it was supposed to do, it kept coming right back up again. When Jeannie and Gloria finally got the end of the snake under the porcelain part where the water and stuff went when you flushed it, it just came back out again.

"Well, that's not bad," Gloria said. "I saw my father fixing our toilet one day, and he said that when the snake comes right back like that, it means that whatever's stopping it up is right near the top."

"What did he do then?" Jeannie asked.

"He used to stick his hand down there and feel around," Gloria said.

"In the toilet?" Jeannie made a face.

"Yeah," Gloria said, making the same kind of face.

"Yuk!" That's what Jeannie said, and I said the same thing. Then Gloria got another idea.

"But he had real long arms so he could do it," she said, looking at me.

"You mean," I said, "that girls don't want to get their hands dirty!"

"You see any rubber gloves around?" Gloria asked. Only now her voice had gotten really small.

There were some rubber gloves on the hamper, and she

put them on. Then she took a breath and started putting her hand all the way down the john.

"Don't be making faces, Jeannie!" Gloria said as her arm went into the toilet past the elbow.

Jeannie was looking at her with her face completely screwed up, and she really looked funny.

"Suppose you find something nasty in there," said Jeannie.

"Like what?" I asked, even though I knew I shouldn't.

"Like some"—she hunched her shoulders up and held her nose—"you know."

"Will you shut up, Jeannie!" Gloria's eyes were glistening a little, like she was on the verge of crying or something, but she still fished around in the john for whatever it was that was stopping it up.

"Don't stir it up too much," Jeannie said.

I wanted to laugh because it really looked funny. There's Gloria on her knees with her hand in the john and her face screwed up one way, and Jeannie standing next to the john with her face screwed up another way. Normally I wouldn't have laughed because I didn't want her to tell me to stick *my* hand down the john. Normally, but then Jeannie had to open her mouth again.

"Say, Gloria," Jeannie said, peering into the water where Gloria's hand had disappeared. "Suppose something grabs your hand."

Well, that cracked me up, and I just about fell down laughing. I looked at Jeannie, and she was trying to keep from laughing, and the tears that Gloria had been fighting came pouring down, but she still kept her hand in the water.

All this really ticked Gloria off and she stood up and told Jeannie that it did.

"Go ahead, you can help," Gloria said. "You give it a try."

Jeannie took a long look at the toilet and then her nose wrinkled up.

"I think this whole idea is ridiculous!" she said. "I'm not putting my hand in any you-know-what!"

"That's what it's all about," Gloria said. "If you're going to be part of this group you have to—"

Gloria hadn't even finished what she was saying before we lost another member of the Action Group. Jeannie slammed the Robinsons' door as she left.

Just then Tina came back and asked us what we were doing. Gloria said that we were trying to unstop the john.

"That ain't the part that's stopped up," Tina said. "It's the top part that's stopped up."

"Then how come all this water is in the bottom part?" Gloria asked.

" 'Cause that's how I found that the top part didn't work," Tina said. "I poured some soapy water in there to wash it out like I do every week, and then I let it sit for a while, and then when I went to flush it it didn't flush."

I got up on the top and looked in and saw that the round ball in the box was caught up against a piece of coat hanger someone had put there before to fix something, and I just gave it a little push. When I did, it started filling up, and a moment later it flushed. Tina said thanks, and then she asked Gloria did she always play in the water like that, and

Gloria got mad even though Tina was only kidding around. It was funny, though.

We got downstairs and a few minutes later Chris's father came by. We had never met Chris's father before. As a matter of fact, we didn't know a whole lot about any of his family. They weren't well off—we knew that, but that was about all we did know. They weren't exactly standoffish, but they weren't what you would call particularly friendly, either. Chris would do things for people, though. He would help someone on the block with a package, or help you fix your bike—that kind of thing. And you would think that you were getting to know him a bit, and then he would almost disappear. Not disappear, really, just never be around the way most of us were. You saw Chris and he was always *going* someplace. He was on his way to school or to the library or to one of the jobs he always seemed to have.

I had been going to school with him for as long as I remember. We were in the third grade together and then again in the first year of junior high. After that I saw him in different classes, but we never had the same home room.

I didn't know his father, either. That is, if I saw him on the street I would speak, and if you asked me who that was I would say that it was Chris's father, but he never stopped to talk to us or anything.

So, when he showed up in front of The Joint I was surprised. I was even more surprised when he sat down. We talked about this and that, and Bubba said he was sorry about the trouble Chris was in and that he was sure everything would be okay. Chris's father said he was sure it would be. Then he asked us if we knew or had heard anything about the robbery. I felt he had wanted to say that all the time but didn't know how to get around to it.

"We've decided to keep our ears and eyes open," I said. "We figure we might be able to hear something that would help."

"Yeah," Bubba said, "we're working on the case. We'll probably solve it before the police will."

"Umm! That's okay." Chris's father rubbed his knee as he spoke. "That's okay. Look, if you hear about anything, let me know. I told my boss about what happened."

He stopped talking, as if he had said something that we should know about. Bubba gave me a look and I gave him one back. I got the impression that Chris's father wasn't too bright.

"We'll let you know if we hear anything," I said.

"Um, yeah, my boss is okay. He's a white guy but he's okay." He was rubbing his knee again. I don't even think he knew he was doing it. "He saw that I was upset, you know, and he ask me what was wrong and I told him. He said it would be a good thing to go around and ask everybody if they heard anything. Then he said he'd put up a thousand dollars if anybody came up with something that would clear Chris."

"Chris is part of the block," I said. "If we hear anything that will help him, we'll let you know. We couldn't take money for helping a friend."

He thanked us and then he changed the subject for a while. Then he said he had to get home and change his clothes. He said it as if it was something we should know about. Then he left.

"I don't think he's wrapped too tight," Bubba said after Chris's father was out of hearing range.

"He's probably just upset," I said. I didn't think he was wrapped that tight myself, but I didn't like talking about it.

"You think his boss is really going to put up a thousand dollars?" Bubba asked.

"Probably," I said. "But you don't need a reward to help a friend."

"No, that's right," Bubba said. "But if he tied me down and stuck it in my pocket against my will, I could live with it."

# CHAPTER
# 5

THERE ARE THINGS PEOPLE ARE SUPPOSED TO LOOK LIKE. Even if people go around saying you shouldn't judge a book by its covers and things like that, you still expect people to look a certain way. You meet a guy who teaches English and he wears glasses. Just about all guys who teach English wear glasses. You see a guy who works in a drugstore and he's usually kind of skinny and he never wears a beard. Guys who play baseball can wear beards and get by, even guys who work in construction, but never a guy who works in a drugstore, and, most important, landlords are supposed to be adults. Anyway, all that was to get into Mr. Pender. We figured that the reason we were having trouble with The Joint was that we were really young, and older people don't know how to deal with young people. They always feel they have to tell us to do something.

So what we did was to think about getting someone to work for us who was a bona fide adult. Then Dean said we should get someone who could do something, too. That seemed like a good idea, and we thought about it for a while. Gloria said we should get someone who could do plumbing, and I thought about getting someone who could help keep the place clean. Bubba said we should get someone to keep the money straight, and that seemed to be the best idea. So we called around to a couple of places from the Yellow Pages to see about hiring an accountant. They were all either not interested or too expensive. Then we called the New York State Employment Service, and after talking to some woman for about five minutes, convincing her that it wasn't a prank call just because we were young, she said she would refer someone to us. Well, who she referred was Mr. Pender.

Mr. Pender was short and very neat. He wore a gray suit that looked very spiffy, and he carried a briefcase. Me and Gloria were in the renting office when he arrived. He didn't look like an accountant to us. In fact, he looked like an ad for tea or something.

"Mr. Williams, please," he said, as he came into the renting office.

"I'm Mr. Williams," I said.

"Pender," he said, "Jonathan Pender, and I'm here to see about the position you have available in your accounting department."

I took a look at Gloria, and she looked at me, and there

was just a little bit of a smile on her face.

"Well, the job is to be the accountant of this building," I said. I started to get up, but then I sat back down again because I thought I would look more important sitting behind the desk.

"And my duties would be?" Mr. Pender's left eyebrow went up about one inch when he asked the question.

"Mostly just accounting stuff," Gloria said. "Do you know how to do that?"

"Yes, as a matter of fact I'm quite good at it," Mr. Pender said. "I am experienced and have references. Am I to take it that you are the owner of this building?"

"Both of us are," I said, "plus a couple of others."

"I see," Pender said. "And who has been keeping your books to this point?"

"What books?" Gloria asked. I was going to say that I was, but Gloria spoke up first.

Mr. Pender said that he "saw" again, and I was just about ready to give up on him and the idea of hiring an accountant altogether. Then Bubba came in, which was no help, and he started in right away about how the block association had come to him and asked for a donation to beautify the block.

"I said okay, right?" Bubba went on. "Then when I gave them twenty cents, they come talking about how they weren't looking for no twenty cents and how they thought I was supposed to be some big-deal landlord."

"Humph!" Gloria tried to draw Bubba's attention to Mr. Pender, who was still standing in the middle of the floor. To me, he looked like a black Charlie Chaplin or somebody.

"So I said, 'If you don't want my twenty cents, give it on back!' And you know, they gave it back?" Bubba said.

"Hey, man, this is Mr. Pender," Gloria said, jumping in when Bubba was catching his breath. "He's an accountant."

"Quite, my friend," said Mr. Pender. "You must be one of the owners."

"Yeah," Bubba said, looking at Mr. Pender suspiciously.

"The job doesn't pay a lot," I said.

"Well, it isn't a very large building," said Mr. Pender. "So I don't imagine it will take my full time to maintain a set of books for you. But I am interested in the position if it is still available."

"You are?" Gloria asked. "I mean, that's great."

We were all smiling because we had an accountant and we were pretty sure that it would make everything a lot easier.

"Of course," Mr. Pender continued, "I imagine my hire would be subject to the approval of the other owners."

I said that I approved and so did Bubba. Mr. Pender said that he was sure that we could work out the terms, and everyone was happy. We all shook hands, and Mr. Pender said that he had some matters to attend to and would return in the morning. Gloria said that we would look forward to seeing him in the morning.

"Well," Mr. Pender said, smiling. "Peerio! Chip, chip, peerio!"

"Wha-?" Bubba looked at Mr. Pender, who was just about to leave. And then, just before he left, Mr. Pender repeated what he had said.

"Peerio! Chip, chip, peerio!" Then he was gone.

We looked at each other after he had left, and then Bubba started laughing. When Bubba laughs, he has three gears. The first gear is when he kind of shouts at you and then the shout breaks up into a laugh. The second gear is when he points at you and then starts stamping his feet. And the third gear is when he falls on the floor and starts rolling around and pointing at the ceiling. When he does this, a real high laugh comes out of him. When Mr. Pender left, Bubba went right into his third gear.

Gloria started laughing, too, and I guess I laughed a little bit.

"Maybe it's English," I said.

We got some pizza and were sitting around with nothing much to do when the phone rang and it was the lady from the employment service. She asked if Mr. Pender had shown up, and we said yes and that he was going to start work for us the next day. She seemed real surprised. I asked her if he was any good, and she said that he was but he was kind of strange, too.

Well, it didn't turn out so bad when he showed up the next day, because he didn't say anything really strange. Not right away, anyway, unless you want to consider that chip, chip, peerio kind of strange. I mean, it's a little *strange,* but it's not too bad once you get used to it. Try saying it aloud sometime, it sounds okay. Only, until you really get it down pat say it when you're by yourself.

"Who did you work for before?" Gloria asked.

"Well, now, that's quite a good question," Mr. Pender said. He was wearing the same suit he had on the day before, and it looked like the same shirt, too, but it was really clean and everything.

"I have been employed with a number of firms as well as my own investment concern," Mr. Pender said. "I have also worked for a number of nonprofit agencies."

"You have your own investment business?" Gloria asked.

"Indeed." Mr. Pender took off his jacket, and we saw that there were rubber bands around his arms just below the elbow, as if his shirt was too long. "My company has been in operation for nearly four years."

"Have I ever heard of your company?" Gloria asked.

To tell you the truth, I was getting tired of Gloria asking all the questions. Mostly because they made her sound as if she was really smart, or at least smarter than me and Bubba. She probably was smarter than Bubba.

"I would imagine not," said Mr. Pender. He was taking yellow pads and pencils out of his briefcase. "But the assets of Financial Banana have more than doubled during its rather short existence."

"Did you say Financial Banana?"

Tina Robinson had come in just when Mr. Pender was talking, and she gave him a quick lookover. Meanwhile Bubba was cracking up again, only this time he was doing it without making any noise. He was in a silent gear three.

"Yes, yes, of course." Mr. Pender looked down at Bubba. "You must be wondering why I call it Financial Banana."

"Yeah, run it on by me," Tina said.

"Well, for the first part it's not a name that one easily forgets, therefore partially eliminating the need for extensive advertising. Secondly, it's an apt name because I invest in fruit futures."

"And you think bananas have a future?" Tina looked real serious.

"That I do, my dear," Mr. Pender said, smiling. "That I do."

You ever find someone you want people to like? Like you find a friend who wears really thick glasses and has big ears or something like that, and right away you start telling people how smart they are or what a nice person they are? Well, for some reason that's the way I felt about Mr. Pender.

I figured if he was working with us, even part time, he couldn't be doing that well, and he seemed like a nice kind of guy. Strange, but a nice kind of guy. I didn't mind Bubba cracking up on him, because Bubba would crack up on anyone. But I didn't like Tina doing a number on him, and I could kind of tell that Mr. Pender didn't either. So I asked Tina what she wanted, and she said she wanted someone to change a light bulb, and then maybe she'd go upstairs and talk to her banana about its future. She winked at Gloria and then left.

"Don't worry about Tina," I said. "She's always shooting her mouth off."

"Oh, I'm not in the least worried," Mr. Pender said. "I've managed to get by the first two thousand years or so, and I imagine that the rest won't be as difficult."

This time even Gloria cracked up a little, but she put her arm around Mr. Pender's shoulder for a moment and gave the guy a squeeze, and then she left. She liked him, too, I thought, and that made me feel glad.

I gave Mr. Pender what records we had, including a composition book that, I assumed, was part of "the books." He started looking them over and sorting them out on the desk.

"I'm really kind of surprised you decided to take the job," I said after everyone else had left. "It's not the greatest job in the world."

"Surprised?" Mr. Pender looked up at me. "Well, yes, you would be, wouldn't you? Do you mind if I ask you whether or not you're religious?"

"Yeah, I'm kind of . . ." I started to say that I was kind of religious, but then I was afraid he was going to ask me what church I went to or something and I didn't want to get into that. "I'm not too religious, but I am a little, if you know what I mean."

"Well, even if you're just a little religious, I think you'll relate to this story," he said. "When Christ was being crucified there were two people, a father and his young son, watching as Christ was carrying the cross up the hill. The little boy asked his father why Christ carried the cross on the shoulder that he did, instead of on the other shoulder the way he had seen his father carry heavy bundles. The father said that every man has his own way of carrying his burdens.

"Now, I don't mean to say that I have a cross to bear or anything of the sort. But I've had to learn to accommodate to life, while you, as a young man, are still trying to get life to accommodate to you. And I won't say you won't be successful. But some men drink, if that is their nature. Some men accumulate wealth or power, if that becomes possible for them, and some merely suffer silently on. I have chosen a compromise which I can tolerate without completely giving up my illusions. Some will find it silly, others amusing, or perhaps deceitful. Still others will find it simply distinctive of me. What more can a man ask for?"

He started going through the papers again, as if the conversation was over, asked a few more questions, gave out a few more "my, *my*'s," and seemed to be really enjoying what he was doing. I left him to his work. I didn't exactly go for the story he was saying, about how everyone had to do their own thing, so to speak, but I still liked him.

I went home, and my father was there and asked me if I wanted to go fishing and I told him no and he asked me why.

"I don't know, I just don't want to go," I said.

"Do you know that you don't want to go?" he said.

"Yeah," I said, knowing the next thing he was going to say.

"Then you ought to know why you don't want to go."

"It's just not my idea of something to do," I said.

He went off in a huff and sat in the dining room and I went to my room. Mom came in with a sandwich, which I wanted to refuse to show that I was pissed, but it was a hamburger with onions so I just chewed it hard instead.

I got two calls within one minute, which was about the first time that had ever happened to me in my life. The first call was from Mr. Pender, and he said that he had put together a temporary set of books and that I could come take a look at them if I wanted to. I didn't really want to, but I figured it was expected of me, so I said I'd be right over. The other call was from Bubba—who else?—and he asked me if

I wanted to take a walk with him. He had his cousin's dog for a week while his cousin went to North Carolina, and he had to take it for a walk.

I met Bubba downstairs and told him about the call from Pender, and I could tell that he wasn't really interested in going to see the books but he felt he had to the same as I did. By now I was a little sorry about having the building. Not that I didn't like the idea, but I was afraid that if we fouled it up my father was going to stick his mouth in it.

Oh, yeah, the dog was crazy.

"His name is Blade," Bubba said. "I think he's a little nervous about being in Manhattan."

"Where's he from?"

"Brooklyn."

He wasn't nervous, he was just crazy. The first thing he did was to run up to a fire hydrant and try to bite it. No lie. He tried to bite it. Bubba pulled him off the fire hydrant, and he stood there and barked at it as if he was really pissed off. You ever see these movies on television where there's an invisible dude walking around doing people dirt, and nobody can see him, and then a dog comes up and starts barking at him? Well, that's what this looked like.

Actually I thought maybe there was some kind of weird smell on the fire hydrant until we got to the tree. He attacked the tree, too. He tried to bite it and he was growling and carrying on. He didn't bother people, but any kind of thing that couldn't move, like a tree, a fire hydrant, or a light pole, really seemed to tick him off.

We got to The Joint and found Pender waiting for us in the office. He showed us the books he set up, and it seemed so logical that I was wondering how come I hadn't thought of it myself. Bubba headed back home, and I walked Pender to the subway station. Seemed he lived in Queens someplace, near Rego Park. He said that he was glad to be working with us.

"I don't really see why," I said. "We seem to be getting all the benefits."

"Only the more obvious ones," he said.

Then I started telling him about how we had thought about setting up books ourselves, which was not really a complete lie, because somebody had mentioned it, I forget who, and how we were sidetracked because of Chris getting arrested.

"This Christopher," Mr. Pender said, "do you think he's really innocent?"

"I'm sure of it," I said. "He's really not that kind of guy. I know it isn't evidence or anything like that, but he's just not the kind of guy to go around stealing like that."

"So," said Pender, "you have two major problems. The first is how to come to terms with Mr. Askia Ben Kenobi—"

"You saw the bill to have the banister replaced?"

"I did, and your notations about how it came to be broken."

"We couldn't think of anything else to do," I said, "so we wrote it all down."

"Not a bad idea," Mr. Pender said. "It's really not a bad idea at all. But I think I might be able to deal with him."

"I wouldn't try it," I said. Askia Ben Kenobi was a good six inches taller than Pender, besides being about twenty-five years younger and a karate expert.

"Well, we'll see," Pender said.

We had reached the subway at 125th Street and St. Nicholas when I remembered that Pender had said we had two problems. I called down the stairs after him.

"Hey, what was the other problem?"

He turned back toward me and then came back up the stairs.

"I suppose you'll be shopping around to see who has the stolen record players and what have you," Pender said. "And I would imagine that finding any kind of stolen merchandise in a city as large as this would be a problem. I imagine, though, that there is someone in the neighborhood who might know where to find a property if the price was right. Wouldn't you?"

I was about to try to stammer out some kind of an answer when Mr. Pender chip-chip-peerioed me, turned, and was gone. It did seem like a good idea. We could let it get around that we were interested in buying some hi-fi equipment and see who turned up with some. It might not work, I knew, but it was worth a try. In fact, it seemed so simple that I wondered why I hadn't thought of it myself.

# CHAPTER
## 6

WE WERE ALL SITTING AROUND THE JOINT THE NEXT DAY
when Mr. Pender showed up. He said that if we wanted him
to he would give us a financial report. Everybody said yes,
which ticked me off just a little. I didn't want to be the boss
or anything, but I thought I did have more of an interest in
The Joint than the others. It didn't even matter to me that it
was my dollar that bought the place or that the building was
actually in my name, although the members of the Action
Group had all signed a paper saying that we all owned The
Joint. Maybe I did want to be the boss—I don't know. I did
know that I was changing the way I felt about owning the
place. And after Mr. Pender's report I was changing even
more.

"I've broken down the costs of owning and operating the building in terms of apartments," Mr. Pender said, rubbing the corner of his mustache with his finger. "The average rent is one hundred and thirty dollars per month per apartment. There are eight apartments being rented, and one, the basement apartment, being exchanged for services.

"It takes the rents from three apartments per year to heat the building and to supply the basic utilities.

"It takes the rent of one apartment to pay the taxes and special assessments, such as sewer and water . . ."

"Sewer and water?" Bubba looked at Mr. Pender. "What sewer?"

"The wastes from the building are emptied into the sewer," Mr. Pender said. "The sewers are maintained by the city, and you have to pay a fee for their use."

"How about the water?" Bubba asked.

"Part of the services you provide when you offer a place for rental," Mr. Pender said. "Shall I go on?"

"Yeah," Bubba said, a little put out.

"Your insurance is equal to a little more than the cost of one and a half apartments. It would be foolish to try to operate a building without insurance. Normal wear and tear, if Mr. Darden does most of the minor repairs, can be kept at one half of one apartment over the cost of the apartment Mr. Darden lives in. Otherwise the cost would be closer to three and one-quarter apartments. Repairs caused by vandalism"—Mr. Pender looked up at us carefully when he said this—"comes to one apartment. That leaves a total profit of one apartment. So what you can expect to earn—that is, if you don't make any improvements in the building, nothing major breaks down, vandalism does not increase, all the apartments are rented and the rent is paid—is the equivalent of one apartment's annual rent."

"Is that a joke?" Gloria asked.

"It's not a joke," Mr. Pender said, "I assure you. The potential for loss is far greater than the potential for profit."

"We oughta find the apartment we're making money on and dump the rest," Bubba said.

"Suppose we raise the rents?" I asked.

"Then you will probably get more people falling behind in their monthly obligations," Mr. Pender said.

"Then there's no way to make money on the building at all," Gloria said. "That's why Harley gave it to us."

"Well, there is a way to possibly make a small profit," Mr. Pender said. "If vandalism is decreased somewhat, it would help. Also, if rents were paid on time, and could be counted on to be paid on time, then some of the moneys realized could be used to make some improvements, which would justify a small raise in the rents."

"We could just double the rents and get better people in here," Bubba said.

"Yeah." Dean hadn't been saying anything, but he was writing down what Pender had said and adding up the figures. "Then we could make about two hundred and sixty a month pure profit."

"Not really—"

"Yes, we could," Dean interrupted. "Because if we're making one apartment profit, that's one thirty per month, right? Then if we doubled the rent, we could pay the same things for taxes and stuff and for the dumb sewer and probably make more money even if the apartments weren't completely filled up."

Dean showed Mr. Pender the paper he had been writing his figures on, and Mr. Pender looked them over carefully.

"The only problem, sir"—Mr. Pender put Dean's paper down—"is that what determines the rent of a building is not simply what you decide to charge. There are a lot of empty places on this block. There's a place on the other side of the street that's boarded up. If you raise the rent by the amount you mention here, people will simply not live here. They will live in an empty apartment across the street or in the next block. Of course, if you could manage to take this building down to the Murray Hill district, you could probably charge more for the apartments. If Mr. Farley could have charged more—"

"Mr. Harley," Bubba corrected.

"If Mr. Harley could have simply charged more, he would have. Your one advantage is that none of you are looking on this place as a sole means of income. You can afford to see what you can do with the building. If you were really good businessmen you would give it up."

"You mean abandon the building?"

"No, I don't," Mr. Pender said. "I don't think inhumanity is ever something that one should do, and abandoning a building is largely inhumane if there are tenants living in it. But once the building was empty you wouldn't want it as a business investment, would you?"

What Pender had said was discouraging, but the profit didn't seem so bad once you thought about it in cash money. It might not have made a lot of money as far as a business went for adults, but for us it wasn't too bad. Only, I wanted to make improvements, and so did the others. We didn't say too much in front of Pender, but we were pretty discouraged when we talked about it among ourselves later.

"Suppose we ran a nonprofit business," Bubba said. "That way we wouldn't have to worry about it."

"You mean, like a hobby?" Dean asked.

"Sure, why not?" Bubba said, liking his own idea. "Then we can just keep it and be landlords."

"And call ourselves the Inaction Group," Gloria said. "Every person who has a house like this has the same problem, and half the people want to walk away from it or just take what little they can. We have to at least try to do better. Maybe we can do something about the people messing up the place."

"Everybody doesn't mess the place up," I said. "Just a few people."

"Yeah, like Askia Ben Kenobi," Bubba said.

# CHAPTER
## 7

WE HAD ALWAYS KNOWN THAT DEAN WAS STRANGE. NOT stupid strange, but weird strange. You ever read about those old guys who just about invented the airplane? Or the guys who first knew about the atoms and how they would blow up the world one day, only they couldn't do anything about it because it was like three thousand years before the first calendar? Dean was one of that kind of guy. He did weird things that weren't quite weird enough to be really weird but were weird enough to be *kind* of weird. For example, he had this goldfish that he was going to try to teach to walk on the ground. So every day he would come home and take the goldfish out of water and hold it up in the air for a few seconds. He said he was speeding up the evolutionary process.

Bubba said if he did that—got the fish to walking around out of water—the fish would probably think that Dean was God and start worshiping him.

"After a while there'd be this funny-smelling church with all fish in the pews worshiping Dean," Bubba said. He also said that he wouldn't want any fish worshiping him.

But that's not the main point. Because it was kind of a way-out idea, but it wasn't that way-out. Suppose you could speed up evolution. It could just work out.

Then another time Dean painted a bottle black and put tape on it and took it outside in the sunlight. He opened the bottle so that light could get in, and then he closed it real tight. Then all of us went up to his house and sat in his room with all the lights out while he opened the bottle to see if we could see any light coming out. We tried it five times, and only once did anybody ever see anything, or think they saw something. That was Florencia. She said she saw a picture of a cowboy. Dean thought that maybe he had trapped some light from the past or something.

To make a long story short, Dean read this book about the power of the mind. He read where some guy from Israel, or some place in that part of the world, could bend nails with his mind. The whole point, the guy said, was that you could do anything you wanted to with your mind, including physical things like moving things around. So what Dean decided to do with his mind was to put an invisible shield around himself and put Askia Ben Kenobi out.

"You sure this invisible shield is going to work?" Gloria said.

"You don't believe it, right?" Dean was rocking back and

forth and humming to himself between his words. "You don't believe it, right?"

"How come you humming?" Gloria said. "I didn't mean any harm."

"He's concentrating his powers of the mind," Bubba said. "You know that aura that Askia Ben Kenobi is always talking about?"

"Yeah?"

"Well, that's the same kind of aura that Dean's putting around himself."

We watched Dean for a while, humming and rocking back and forth. Then all of a sudden he bolted out the door and up the stairs toward Askia's apartment. We followed, but it was hard to keep up with him. By the time we had made it to the third floor, Dean was already banging on Askia Ben Kenobi's door.

"NNNnmmmmmmm!" And he was humming. He banged some more and did some more humming. "NNNNNnnnnnnnn!"

Askia Ben Kenobi threw open the door. He was all greased up again and had a silver star hung around his neck.

"Who knocks upon the door of Askia Ben Kenobi?" Askia Ben Kenobi said. I never noticed it before, but his nose moved when he breathed just like Brock Peters' nose did.

"AAAiiieeee!"

When Dean screamed, Askia Ben Kenobi jumped back and went into his karate stance. All his fingers were pointing toward Dean, and his teeth were clenched.

"AAAiiieeee!" Dean said it again, except this time it

wasn't so much of a screech as it was a little noise that he made. "OOOOiiiii! EEeedebeedeee! Wahoooooo! Bee-wooooo!"

Each time Dean would make a new noise, he would go into another pose. They weren't exactly karate poses, but more a cross between ballet and the way you look when you follow through in bowling. Anyway, he kept making the noises, each one a little softer than the last, and then he started down the stairs. We all watched him, including Askia Ben Kenobi. But Dean went on down the stairs, making those little noises and posing. I looked up at Askia, and he shrugged and went back into his apartment.

"What happened?" I asked when we got back downstairs and found Dean sitting in the office.

"Yeah, I thought you were going to put him out," Bubba said.

"What happened to your shield?" Gloria asked.

"The shield was there," Dean said. "Only it was just around my mind. I was afraid he was going to kick my rear end. Got to figure a way to get that shield a little lower."

"You mean you chickened out?" Bubba asked.

"Would you believe I was afraid I might hurt him?" Dean asked.

"No," Bubba said, "I wouldn't. I think you chickened out!"

"That," said Dean, "is the way it be's sometime."

It seemed that we were going to have to learn to live with Askia Ben Kenobi.

74

# CHAPTER

I WAS BORN IN MARCH AND I'M AN ARIES, AND BUBBA WAS born in May and he's a Taurus. I don't believe in signs or anything like that, but I thought I'd throw that out so you know, and if you believe in signs you'll know what I mean next. Also, my biorhythms are completely different than Bubba's. I'm thin, at least thinner than he is, and I think I'm better looking except for my ears, which are little and just a bit pointed at the top. Which doesn't mean a thing, no matter what anyone says. Anyway, the fact that me and Bubba are different didn't stop us both from being zapped on the same day.

Bubba got zapped first. He had contacted the Captain and

told him that he wanted to be a numbers runner. Now the Captain is the main numbers man in the neighborhood. He is very fat, with little pig eyes that are always blinking, and short little fingers that are always a little greasy, I guess from the way he eats.

When Bubba told the Captain he wanted to be a numbers runner, the Captain told him to come over to where he stayed, which was the back of a dry cleaner's store, and take the numbers runner test. He was supposed to come over at exactly three o'clock that afternoon. The Captain said that anybody else who wanted to be a numbers runner could come over, too. Bubba said that he wanted to be a numbers runner mostly because he wanted to be two things in life—rich and cool. As far as we could tell, the Captain was rich—he was always flashing a big roll of money. When he gave somebody some money, he would never look at the money. He would look right at the person's face and count the money out. First he would lick his thumb, and then he would take a bill from his roll and put it in the person's hand, and then he would lick his thumb again, and then he would take another bill from the roll. Sometimes the roll would have hundred-dollar bills and twenties and tens—still the Captain wouldn't look at it. They said he never made a mistake.

So when the Captain said for Bubba to come over and take the numbers runner test, Bubba figured he wanted to see if he could count.

"Fifty-sixty-seventy-eighty-ninety-one-oh-five—" Bubba rattled off. He was practicing counting Monopoly money in the office. I was helping him, and Mr. Hyatt, who lives in 2A and who was now a little tipsy, was watching.

"Whose picture is on a ten-dollar bill?" Mr. Hyatt asked.

"I don't know," Bubba said.

"Well, you better find out," Mr. Hyatt said. "One time I was applying for a job in the bank across from Smilen Brothers, and they asked me whose picture was on a ten-dollar bill. I didn't know whose picture was on no ten-dollar bill and I didn't get the job."

"Whose picture is on the ten-dollar bill?" I asked.

"Thomas Jefferson's," Mr. Hyatt said. He seemed proud that he knew.

Then we tried to find out whose pictures were on all the bills, and we only got a few of them. But it was getting to be time to go over to the dry cleaner's, and me and Bubba and Dean went over.

Weasel was out front in the dry cleaner's. He just sat in a chair behind the counter and looked mean. That was his job. He was big and ugly and mean looking. When you went in to see about getting your clothes out of the cleaner, he would look at you like you had said something about his mother or something. They said that he had a gun and would shoot you if you sneezed wrong.

"We're supposed to see the Captain," Bubba said to Sally. Sally was the girl who worked behind the counter.

Sally looked over at Weasel and Weasel looked at Bubba. Bubba tried to smile, but it came out like he was making a face or something, and he looked away. Then Weasel looked at me and Dean, and we looked away, too.

Then he nodded and Sally let us go into the back where the Captain was sitting drinking coffee and listening to the radio.

"Hi!" Bubba said.

"How much is twenty-seven times nine?" the Captain asked.

"What?" Bubba looked at him.

"That ain't the right answer," the Captain said. "Try again."

"What were those numbers again?"

"Twenty-seven times nine!"

"Nine times seven is what?" Bubba scratched his head. "Is sixty-three. Nine times two is eighteen. One eighty-three, and six left over is one nine."

The Captain reached over on a shelf and pulled down a paper and pencil.

"Do it right this time."

When Bubba did it again, it came out to two hundred and three.

"Write down two hundred and three on this paper," the Captain said, giving Bubba another piece of paper.

Bubba wrote it down.

"Now here's a dollar for you to play that number for me, okay?"

"Okay." Bubba smiled.

"See, you too dumb to keep the numbers in your head and figure them out like a good numbers man, so you got to write them down on a paper. I'll tell you how to play it soon as I finish this here coffee."

The Captain kept his little pig eyes right on Bubba as he slurped down his coffee.

"Captain, here come that cop again!" It was Sally from the front.

"Ball that piece of paper up real quick!" the Captain said to Bubba.

Bubba balled the sheet of paper up as fast as he could and looked around for someplace to throw it. He started to throw it in the wastepaper basket, but the Captain stopped him.

"That'll be the first place they look," he said. "Put it in your mouth. If they find you with that paper, you'll be in jail before you turn around."

We could hear footsteps coming toward the back just as Bubba got the paper in his mouth.

"Swallow it, quick!" the Captain said.

Just then two cops, one white and the other one black, came in with Sally.

"What you doing, Mr. Lloyd?" the white cop asked.

"You call me Captain like everybody else," the Captain said.

"What these boys doing here?" the black cop asked. He poked me with his stick. "What's your name?"

"Paul Williams," I said. I tried to look over to where the Captain was sitting, to see how he was taking the whole thing, but I couldn't get my eyes to move right.

"What's your name?" the black cop asked Dean next.

"Who, me?"

"Yeah, you."

"Me?" Dean's eyes were as wide as saucers.

"Yeah, you are standing here, ain't you?" the cop asked.

"Dean Michaels." The voice that came out of Dean sounded completely different than the way he usually sounds.

"And how about you, my man?" The white cop tapped Bubba on the end of his nose, and Bubba made a sound like a frog.

"Hey, this one's real funny," the white cop said. "You tap him on his nose and he makes a sound like a frog."

The white cop tapped Bubba on his nose, and he made a sound like a frog again. Then I realized what he was doing. He was trying to swallow that piece of paper that the Captain had made him put in his mouth.

"We could put him on *The Gong Show,*" the black cop said. "Now you let me tap his nose, because I got the most rhythm, and you kind of lead him through a tune. We might have us something here."

So the black cop started tapping Bubba on the nose, and the other cop pretended like he was leading an orchestra, and Bubba was making those frog noises, though not like he was making a tune, because you could tell that Bubba was scared. If you didn't know him and couldn't tell by the funny look in his eyes, you could probably tell by the tears running down his cheeks.

"You know"—the white cop turned to the Captain—"you got some funny people hanging out with you. Strange."

Then the two cops left. They weren't gone more than a few seconds when Bubba threw up. He threw up in the wastepaper basket mostly, except for a little bit on his pants and on Dean's sneakers.

"How much is thirty-one times thirteen," said the Captain as Bubba was finishing throwing up in the basket.

Bubba didn't even bother trying to figure that one out. He just got up, wiped his face off on his sleeve, and headed for the door.

"You people sure you the future?" Sally asked as we went through the front.

The more I thought of what had happened, the more I thought that the Captain had set it up. The Captain was really okay, or at least he was as far as I could tell. What he was doing with Bubba was showing him that the whole idea of being a numbers runner was not so cool after all. One of the things that the Captain could have done was to play big man and try to impress us, but he didn't. Instead he just went about the business of what he was about and letting us know that we weren't going to be runners just because we liked the idea.

That's how I got into trouble with Gloria. I figured that what the Captain was doing was being a total businessman. Maybe later on I would have thought differently, but not right then. Bubba went on home and Dean and I went over to The Joint.

"You see this note that Pender left?" Gloria asked when we got to the office.

I hadn't. It said that Askia Ben Kenobi had paid a month's rent and we should think about whether we wanted to accept it or to try to evict him. It also said that Ella

Fox had not paid her rent again and had no immediate prospects.

"This dude she used to be married to came around and said that he got a job and that he needed the money to buy tools, and she like a fool let him have the money," Gloria said.

"What's the matter?" Dean asked. "Does he lie a lot?"

"Do fish swim?" Gloria replied. "Now she's four months behind in the rent, and this guy is probably going off wasting the money."

"Then she's got to go," I said.

"How can she go find this guy when she don't even know where the turkey lives?" Gloria said.

"I didn't mean go find him," I said. "I mean go find someplace else to live."

"You mean *what*?" Gloria turned her head sideways, and her eyes were teary looking.

"Look. Gloria," I said, leaning back in the swivel chair, "this is a business. We're in the business of renting places to people. We have to take care of business or we won't be any better off than she is."

"Can't she get welfare?" Dean asked.

"No, because every time she goes down to the welfare department, they call up this guy and he starts talking about how he sends her money and stuff. Now with the city in a bind and everything, the only thing she gets is what her mother can give her."

"Let her move in with her mother," I said.

"Let her do *what*?" Gloria was really mad now. "Let her do *what*? We're supposed to be some kind of Action Group to do something for people, and here you are talking about the same kind of things everybody else is!"

"It's different running a business than sitting around hoping that everything works out," I said. "What's the right thing to do? You tell me! You want to raise everybody else's rent so they can cover for her? You want to get some part-time jobs so we can run the whole place for nothing? That's why that guy gave us the building in the first place!"

"Right, and why did we take it?" asked Gloria. "Why did we take it? So we could put people out on the street and say what cool people we are? You explain that to her little girl, how cool you are for putting her out on the street!"

"It's not my little girl," I said.

"No, it's not yours—" Gloria was crying.

"There's no need to—"

"It's not your little girl—" Gloria said. "She did it all by herself. It's an immaculate birth so now you can go worship it! Those are the only kinds that men really dig, you know!"

Gloria left, banging her wrist into the side of the door as she did. Me and Dean just sat there for a while, and I felt like about change for two cents.

After a while Petey Darden and Mrs. Darden came in and said hello, and then Mrs. Darden said she was going to go start supper.

"You look like you just lost a friend," Mr. Darden said.

"Argument with Gloria," I said.

"I know, we saw her on the corner," he said. "You decided anything yet?"

"I guess not," I said. "I'm not sure what's right, really."

"Doesn't always make a difference if you do," Mr. Darden said. "Sometimes you think something has two sides and you find out it doesn't, just two different places you can see the same side from. When that happens, right can be wrong and wrong can be right, and the worst thing in the world can be right in the middle. But you knew it wasn't going to be easy, didn't you?"

"No, as a matter of fact, I didn't," I said.

Dean and me went over to the park and played some one-on-one. He won every game, which was nothing new because he always won one-on-one games from me. We played until it started getting dark and then we left the park.

"You think there's going to be any profit from us having this place?" Dean asked.

"You mean money?"

"Yeah."

"I don't know," I said. "I thought we agreed not even to discuss it until we had the place running pretty smoothly."

"Yeah," he said, "I know. But just in case there is some profit, you could use my part for Ella Fox."

He quickly changed the subject and we talked about basketball until we hit the block. He went on home and I went to Gloria's. Her mother kidded me a little—she did that a lot because she liked me—and then she went in to get Gloria. She came out a moment later and told me that I could go into Gloria's room.

Gloria was sitting on the bed and facing away from me as I stood in the doorway. She didn't say anything and neither did I for a while. I liked it better when she was screaming at me.

"I'm sorry," I said. "Maybe we can talk about it again

84

some other time. Dean had an idea that might work out."

"I don't think I want to talk about it any more," she said. "I'm probably not really cut out for this kind of thing."

"You have to admit it's hard to know what's right and what's wrong," I said, thinking of what Mr. Darden had said. "On one hand you have a business to run, which could help people, and on the other hand you feel for people. I mean, even if nothing is clear one way or the other, you have to draw a line somewhere or you'll probably go wrong both places."

"Maybe I shouldn't be in business then," Gloria said, her eyes misting over. "If I have to see people different and feel about them different because I'm in some kind of a business, then I should get out of business. I don't like being wrong any more than anyone else does, but if I'm going to be wrong, then I'm going to be wrong where the people are, not with where the business is!"

I felt bad about what Gloria was saying. I didn't know what else to say to her so I just told her that I would call her in the morning. The truth was that I was beginning to wish I had never seen or heard about The Joint. It would have been easy if I could have come up with some great answer to solve everything. In a way I guess I thought I would—we all thought we would come up with something great and be heroes and all. But it wasn't that simple.

I also didn't want Gloria mad at me, because I was really beginning to like her. Now she was saying things that I knew as well as she did, and I was feeling like the bad guy on the set. If I had had to support a family by making a go of The Joint, I wouldn't have known what to do with myself. As it was, by the time I got home I was exhausted and feeling about as sorry for myself as I ever have. I didn't want to think about how Ella Fox felt. That's true, I just didn't want to think about it at all, but it was just about the only thing I could think of as I lay in the darkness that night.

The next morning when I woke up I checked the newspaper for my horoscope. It just said that I would get along well with a female relative and not to be impatient in matters of the heart. It was silly, but no more so than my looking it up, I suppose. I was beginning to understand people believing in horoscopes or investing their money in numbers when they didn't see any other answers to their problems. But understanding didn't make things any easier.

# CHAPTER

BUBBA CALLED ME ABOUT NINE-THIRTY IN THE MORNING. HE sounded scared.

"You better get down here right away!" he said. "There's some people down here taking over the building. They got television and everything!"

I had one sweat sock on and couldn't find another clean one, and then I couldn't find my other sneaker, so I ran down as quickly as I could in one slipper and one sneaker. I could see the crowd from halfway down the block. There were two big trucks there—one looked like a half truck and half bus and the other was a Volkswagen van. There was a guy standing on the stoop, and he looked really mad about something.

"And what this is all about"—the guy on the stoop had his fist in a tight ball—"is a revolution of the people against the powers that be! Do you hear me? The POWERS that be!"

He looked around, and the people who were watching shifted a little.

"When I say REV-O-LU-TION I mean just that! REV-O-LU-TION! A revolution is a turn. A wheel turns! A wheel turns and they call it a REV-O-LU-TION! And that's what we are here about! Do you hear me?"

"Yeah, we listening," somebody said.

"We here to take over this building from the powers that be! From the slumlords who oppress us. We are here to turn the power! We are here to turn the power from the hands of the oppressor over to the hands of the oppressed!"

"Could some of you people move back a little?" One of the TV cameramen was laying cable along the sidewalk to one of the lights. The other TV people were setting up the stuff that was in the larger truck.

"Let them on through!" the speaker said. "We ain't got nothing to do that we can't let the world see us! I am an oppressed man seeking to regain my rights! To have the rights that God has given me, and which this oppressive society has taken from me and turned over to the slumlords of the ghetto, the gunlords down in the Pentagon, and the funlords in Atlantic City!"

"Go on and preach now!" somebody yelled out.

"Look at this raggedy building that our people are supposed to live in! Look at the busted-up garbage cans and dirt in front of it! Is this where our children are supposed to play? *Is it?*"

"No!" came back the chorus.

"You bet it ain't! But that's where they got to play! And this raggedy building is where our people got to live while the fat landlord lives downtown in a high-rise luxury building and sends his fat wife down to Florida for a suntan!"

"That's the truth!" a woman standing right next to me said.

"And while she's down there soaking up the sun, he's up here sucking up the blood of the poor! I went into this building just a few days ago and saw that the banister was gone! They tell me the banister ain't been there for two years! I am tired to my heart and sick to my soul of these slumlords who don't care two cents for the way we got to live! They want us to live in these rattraps, pay them with our blood, and keep quiet!"

"We ain't keeping quiet!" That was the guy who delivered packages in the grocery store.

"You damn right we ain't keeping quiet!" The guy on the stoop was wiping the sweat from his face. "They want us to keep quiet, but they gonna hear me!"

"Let 'em hear you, brother!"

I couldn't see who said that because I was backing away a little.

"The powers that be don't want to hear my anger!" The guy was really shouting now.

"They even taking down the television stuff!" a woman said.

"Why you taking down the cameras?" the guy on the stoop said. "Does it get to you? Does it make your blood crawl and turn? Does it make you scared?"

"One of the lights is out and there's not enough light on this side of the street to use the color cameras," the TV man said.

"Not enough light?" The guy looked around. "Light is the truth of the world! Light is the truth that I will shed on the oppressor! All the oppressors are the same! Every single one of them!"

He started edging down the steps of The Joint, and then he started walking down the street.

"The revolution needs leaders and that's what I am!" he shouted from the middle of the street. "The REV-O-LU-TION needs leaders who can take the fight to the street. I ain't tied to no one place! No one building! I go where the revolution calls because I do not follow—I lead!"

By that time he was on a stoop across the street and they were setting up the cameras over there. I stayed around long enough to find out that he was taking over that building, not mine. I wondered how much history was made that way.

# CHAPTER
## 1️⃣0️⃣

I HADN'T EXACTLY MADE UP WITH GLORIA, BUT AT LEAST SHE wasn't really mad at me any more. I don't think she was so much mad at me as she was at how things were going down, anyway. When I thought about it later, I realized that what she was saying, about being for people and everything, wasn't going to solve the problems of running the building. It solved the problem of knowing how to feel and of saying something cool, but it was something else again to get the money to run things so that things would be as cool for real as they were in talk.

The next day I went to The Joint, and there was a note there from Tina Robinson. I was sitting in the office wondering what she wanted when the ambulance came. They were coming to take Mr. Hyatt to the hospital.

Any time you saw Mr. Hyatt he was drunk or getting drunk or trying to recover from being drunk. It used to be funny, but after a while it got to be sad, mostly because he would try to make little jokes about it. You could see that he felt bad about it. I asked the ambulance driver what was wrong, and he said that Mr. Hyatt had pneumonia, or at least it looked like he did.

"Mostly when you get a drunk he's either got a bad liver, a heart attack, or pneumonia," the driver said. "I think this guy might have at least two of them."

I asked what hospital they were taking him to, and they said Metropolitan. Just as the ambulance was pulling away from the curb, Gloria came up with Dean and Bubba.

"What happened?" Bubba asked.

"That guy in 2A has pneumonia," I said, taking a look at Gloria. "He'll probably be in the hospital for a couple of weeks."

Bubba started going on about how he had an uncle who had pneumonia, and then Dean chipped in with a cousin. Gloria didn't say anything. I could have gone on about who was going to pay the rent on that apartment, but I didn't.

We went into the office, and I told Dean and Bubba about the note, and Dean went up to see Tina. Me and Bubba split a soda and talked about a track meet that was coming up soon, and Gloria said she was going out to take a walk. She came back before Dean did, with two containers of tea. She asked me if I wanted one and I said no. Dean came back and said that the doorknob on Tina's bathroom door was broken.

"How can you break a doorknob?" I asked.

"It's not really broken," Dean said. "It just doesn't turn the latch. You turn it and it just keeps turning around."

"All you got to do is tighten the screw in the doorknob, and then you can turn it."

"I know," Dean said. "I tried to turn it with a dime, but it didn't turn far enough."

"I'll take a screwdriver and go up and do it," Gloria said.

"I told Pender about Chris," I said.

"What did my man say?" Bubba asked. "Chip, chip, peerio?"

"You know, I think he's cool," Gloria said. "He's kind of funny, but he's okay in a funny kind of way."

"Anyway, he had a good idea," I said. "Let's go around and tell people that we're in the market for a stereo set. Then, if anyone knows where the stolen stuff is, maybe they'll come up and say that it's for sale."

"That was Mr. Pender's idea?" Dean asked.

I nodded.

"That's not bad, but who do we tell?" Bubba asked.

"How about A.B.?" Gloria asked.

A. B. Tucker had a real name. I think it was something like James or Joe or something like that, but he told everybody to call him A. B. He was watching a football game once between a team from Texas and a team from Arkansas, and half the players didn't have real names, just initials. One guy was named B. B. something or other, and another guy was R. D. Something or other, stuff like that. So A. B. took those initials. He would usually get mad if you called him by his first name, which I forget, and tell you to call him by those initials. A. B. used to sell stuff. He said it was all hot stuff, but I don't think anybody could steal that much stuff. He used to brag that if you wanted something, all you had to do was to tell him where they kept it and he'd get it for you.

"Look, why don't you and Dean go over and tell A. B. that we're looking for some stereo equipment—"

"To put into the lobby to give The Joint some class," Dean said. "Then he won't think we're just trying to find out who stole it."

"Yeah," I said. Dean didn't have a lot of good ideas, but when he did have one it was really good.

So Dean and Bubba went out to find A. B. and left me and Gloria in the office. I didn't say anything, and I could tell she was getting a little nervous.

"I guess you're wondering how we're going to get money up if nobody pays their rent," she said.

I shrugged. That was one thing I was wondering. The other thing was how I got into the real-estate business in the first place.

"I have an idea," Gloria said. "You sure you don't want some tea?"

"It's too hot for tea," I said. "Since when did you start drinking tea?"

"I read in biology that if you drink warm liquids it'll cool you off more than cold liquids."

"Does it?"

"No." She smiled, and that broke the tension between us a little. "You want to hear my idea?"

"Sure."

"Let's raise some money from someplace else," she said, opening the second container of tea. "Then while Mr. Pender gets his act together with the books and everything, at least we can hang on long enough to find out the right thing to do about The Joint."

"How we going to raise the money?"

"I thought about a street fair," Gloria said. "We could have the whole block come and then maybe we could pay off some of the bills that we have, and—you know—"

"We wouldn't have to talk about putting anyone out?"

"Right."

"Well, let's think about it," I said. "You want me to go up with you to fix Tina's doorknob?"

She said okay, and we got a screwdriver and started up. On the way we joked a little about how Tina always had something wrong with her bathroom, Mrs. Jones on the first floor always had her lights blowing out, and Mr. Lowe on the top floor was always complaining about how the halls were dirty. To tell the truth, I think we were both getting a little discouraged.

"It's about time you people showed up," Tina said. She had one of those round powder puffs and was spreading powder all over her face. Tina wasn't the best-looking woman in the world without the powder—with the powder she looked as if she just died and hadn't gotten around to laying down.

"Slam the door when you leave," she said, stuffing the powder puff into a handbag as she went through the door. "And fix that doorknob right!"

I handed the screwdriver to Gloria and sat on the edge

of the tub as she tightened the screw.

"You know, the worst thing about this is that I hate to give up," Gloria said. "You know what I mean?"

"I guess so."

"People are always talking about slumlords and people deserting their buildings and everything—"

"We didn't ask for The Joint," I said. "We kind of inherited it, so to speak."

"Yes, but if we can't find a way to do something, then what can we say about the people who do just take the money and run?"

"I don't know," I said.

Gloria kept working on the doorknob, and I took a look in Tina's medicine cabinet. There were more little bottles and tubes in that cabinet than I had ever seen before. Half the bottles were so old that the labels were yellow. She had everything from hair dye to skin creams and some things that didn't look like anything I had ever seen. There was one tall jar with a thick green liquid in it and something floating around in it. I took the top off and smelled it. Horrible.

"What's this?" I asked Gloria.

She looked at it and shook her head. She was leaning against the door and really trying to get the screw tight enough. Now, I'm not against women's lib or anything like that, but I think men are better at fixing things than women. I didn't say anything to Gloria and just waited. She took a little look at me, knew what I was thinking, and really started working with the screwdriver.

"Here." She handed me the screwdriver and sat down. I looked at her, and she was looking down and sipping on the tea, which she had brought with her.

The screw had come loose in the doorknob. There's a square rod that goes through the door itself and turns when you turn the knob. The knob goes over the square rod and the screw in the shaft of the knob fits against one of the sides of the square rod so that it turns. I took a look at it and started turning it. I gave it two or three easy turns and it turned easily. I couldn't figure why Gloria couldn't have tightened it. Then it turned a few more times, just as easily. I tried unscrewing it and it came out easily. I took a look at it and saw the problem. The threads on the screw had been stripped.

"See here," I said, showing the screw to Gloria, "the threads are stripped. You could turn it all day and you couldn't tighten it."

"Oh," she said. She sounded kind of defeated.

"Look, it's no big thing," I said. "We'll just pick up another one at the hardware store and you can put it in."

She smiled again and I felt better. I began to realize something that had been gnawing at me for a while and that I couldn't put my finger on. I was really beginning to like Gloria. I was feeling pretty good about it, too. The good feeling lasted at least fifteen seconds. Then I tried to get out of the bathroom.

The first thing I tried was just to turn the doorknob. Of course it just spun around. I got an "Oh, no," from Gloria, but I told her it wasn't going to be a problem. I would just take the knob off and turn the square rod. No way. I twisted on the rod until my fingers got sore. Then I had an inspiration. I pushed the doorknob through and tried to turn the latch with the screwdriver. Nothing. Gloria was laughing.

I unscrewed the plate that covered the keyhole. That didn't help at all. Gloria was still laughing.

"We're stuck," I said.

Well, if I liked Gloria a few minutes ago I didn't like her now. That is, I still liked her but I hated the way she was laughing. She was really laughing, and I felt a little bit like a jackass. If I hadn't felt so high and mighty when she couldn't tighten the screw, I wouldn't have felt so low when I found out we were stuck. But we were stuck and so we just sat there.

"Did Tina say when she was coming back?" I asked.

"She said something about going to a party," Gloria said. "She might not be back until one or two o'clock in the morning."

"How about her sister?"

"She's going to meet her at the party."

"You want to call for help?"

"Do *I* want to call for help?"

"I mean, do you think *we* should call for help?"

"You think it would do any good? There's no window in here and we'd have to call through the bathroom door and the outside door. The only other people on this floor is Mr. Hyatt—"

"And he's in the hospital."

"And Ella Fox, and she could be at her mother's."

We sat for a while and didn't say anything. Once in a while when our eyes met I would kind of smile, but she would smile more, almost a laugh, and I wasn't sure if she was laughing because the situation was funny or laughing at me.

"You want to talk about something?" I asked.

"What?"

"Anything'll do."

"Suppose both Tina and Johnnie Mae come home from the party together, see—"

"Yeah."

"And they're crossing Broadway and 129th Street, see—"

"Yeah."

"And a bus pulls out and knocks them both down."

"What kind of talk is that?"

"What would happen to us?"

"What do you mean what would happen to us?"

"What would we do?"

"Somebody would come to look for us after a while," I said.

"Maybe in a month or two, right?"

"Let's change the subject."

"What do you want talk about?" she said.

"Let's talk about the problems with The Joint," I said. "Suppose your street fair idea doesn't work, then what will we do?"

"I don't know," she said. She looked sad.

That wasn't the nicest thing for me to have said, I know, because I knew that Gloria was trying to work out something for The Joint and for the people who lived in it, but right then we were stuck in the bathroom and I was feeling pretty much like a fool and she was seeming to enjoy the whole thing. It was a case of me being uptight and sort of knowing that I was uptight and not being able to get out of it. We didn't say anything else for a long time, and the quiet around us got to be a bit spooky. You could hear a few noises from the street but not many, and occasionally there would be the sound of a scurry in the walls that could have been plaster falling or could have been rats.

"We have another problem," Gloria said. "I didn't want to bring it up before, but now I think I have to."

"What's that?"

"I have to go to the bathroom."

Now it was my turn to laugh and her turn not to like it. I stood up and tried the screwdriver in the door again, but it didn't work this time either. I looked at Gloria and I knew it was serious. She really had to go to the bathroom. That is, we were in the bathroom and she really had to use it.

"I'll turn my back," I said.

"I don't want to go while you're in here," she said.

"Oh. Then you'll have to wait," I said.

"I can't wait."

"Well, what do you want me to do?"

"Turn the light out."

I turned the light out.

"Where are you?" she asked.

"Right here."

"Near the light switch?"

"Yeah."

"Turn it back on."

I turned the light switch back on, and she told me to take the light bulb out of the socket. I unscrewed it carefully and it was dark in the room again. Then she asked me where I was standing, and I was standing in the same place.

"This is embarrassing," she said.

"Why don't you hurry up and get it over with?" I said.

Then she asked me if I was holding the light bulb in my hand, which I was. I started to put it down and it must have fallen into the sink. From the tinkling sound it made I knew she wouldn't be worried about it any more.

"How come you broke the light bulb?"

"What do you mean, how come?" I answered. "Why don't you just finish doing whatever it is you're doing so we can try to get out of here."

"Okay, but don't look."

Don't look. I couldn't see my own hand an inch in front of my face—how was I going to look at her? I did listen, though. But I didn't hear anything.

"You finished?" I asked.

"I don't think I can go," she said.

"I thought you had to go so bad."

"I do, but I can't go with you in the room."

Neither one of us heard Tina come back in the apartment. At least, I didn't hear her anyway. In fact, I jumped a little when her voice came from the other side of the door.

"Who in there?"

"It's me and Gloria," I said. "The doorknob fell off."

"I got it," she said.

"Wait, don't open the door!" Gloria called out.

I had forgotten about Gloria, or at least what she was doing. I heard some rustling about in the dark and I guessed she was getting herself back together.

"What you people doing in there?" Tina called. "You

want me to go away and come back later?"

"No," Gloria called out.

We heard the doorknob being pushed back into the door.

"Not yet! Not yet!" Gloria called out. But the door flew open anyway just in time to catch Gloria pulling up the zipper on her dungarees.

"I didn't know you people were sweet on each other," Tina said as we emerged from the bathroom.

Gloria started stammering out an explanation, but I just left. She caught up with me on the stairs and started yelling at me for not waiting to tell Tina what really happened.

"I was so amazed I didn't even think about it," I said.

"Amazed at what?" Gloria asked, giving me about the worst look I had ever seen.

"Amazed that I could see so well in the dark!" I shouted over my shoulder as I ran down the last flight of stairs.

# CHAPTER
## 11

I ALMOST GOT INTO A NORMAL CONVERSATION WITH MY father. Almost, because, as usual, he turned it into an argument. It started off with me sitting in the living room reading the paper, which by itself is a new thing. My father kept getting on my case about not spending time with the family. What did he say? Oh, yes, "The family is the strongest unit in civilization." One of those semi-cool things that don't make any sense. I mean, what are you going to say? That it's not as strong as a Boy Scout troop? Or a football team? You don't have anything to say, so you just nod and say, "Yeah."

So what I was doing was hanging around for an hour or so before I went to my room. I have a nice room. There were two closets in my room when we first got this apartment. My father fixed up the smaller closet for my clothes and he fixed up the bigger one as an entertainment center. There was a shelf on the top for the television and down below I had a record player, tape recorder, and radio. Everybody who saw it thought it was just out of sight. And there was a sliding door that he built that looked like a bookshelf when you closed it. It was really nice. That's another thing I can't stand about my father. He has these things that he can do and he thinks that everybody can do them if they just tried. Like building the entertainment center out of the closet. He'd say something to me like, "Why don't you build a bird feeder?" And it would seem like a good idea, only after fooling around with some wood for a while, I'd be ready to just make a big sign for the birds telling them where they could pick up some food stamps or something. Then he would make one, and it would look like a castle or some other good-doing thing, and I would just hate it to death. Oh, well, at least I knew what I didn't like about him. Nothing vague.

So it's Friday night and I'm sitting there reading the paper and he turns to me and asks me how Bubba is doing.

"Bubba?" I said. "He's okay."

"And the building?"

"You mean The Joint," I said. "I guess it's okay."

"Are you people still running around trying to convince yourselves that Chris didn't steal anything?"

"Are we still trying to convince ourselves?" I put the paper down. "We don't have to convince ourselves because we know he didn't. Do you mean you still think he stole that stuff?"

"Let's put it this way," he said. "No one has convinced me that he hasn't had a part in it."

I looked at Mom and she had her head down, but I could see she had that little smile on her face that she always got when me and my father got into it.

"You know anything about the Inquisition?" I asked.

"Do you know anything about court costs?" he said.

"What are you talking about?"

"It's going to cost the State of New York thousands of dollars to bring this case to trial," my father said. "And it's not that important a case."

"The guy's whole life can be ruined, but it's not that important a trial," I said, trying to get as much sarcasm in my voice as possible.

"What I mean is that it's not that important to the State," my father went on. "If they didn't have a good case, they wouldn't even bother with bringing it to trial. Nobody was injured. There weren't any firearms involved. They got this guy dead to rights. And he's running around spending money like water. Where'd he get all that money?"

I didn't know what money he was talking about, and I let the conversation peter out.

I thought about what my father had said, which I usually did after we had an argument. He'd get all his stuff in during the argument, and then afterwards I'd think of all the things I should have told him. Only he would have his stuff before he would start the argument and then sneak up on it. That's true. He was like a snake. You would be sitting around, having a conversation, minding your own business, when he would switch it without warning. Like one time I was complaining because I had the lowest allowance of anybody I had ever heard of who had ever lived. My father, besides being stubborn as a mule, is cheap. Cheap isn't even the word. He gives me four dollars a week for an allowance. Nobody in the world gets four dollars a week allowance any more. That's to begin with. Only he gives me two dollars in change (never dollar bills) and two dollars he puts into the bank with a long lecture about how I'm really going to Appreciate It One Day.

I had been complaining about this miserable way of getting my allowance once when we were going down the street near Union Square. I had my two dollars, in change, and was getting pretty ticked off about it when he stops in front of this blind guy. And he says, "Why don't you give your two dollars to this gentleman?"

Well, the whole thing was pretty embarrassing. I mean, there's this blind guy standing there listening to this, and I'm standing there feeling like a dope. I don't want to give away my two dollars, but I don't want the blind guy to feel like a dope, either. So I give this blind guy thirty-five cents. I drop it in his cup.

"That's not two dollars," my father says. And now he's holding me by the arm so I can't walk away, and other people are beginning to give us a look. What do I do? I dropped the whole two dollars in the guy's cup.

Then we walked on.

"You didn't want to give the man your two dollars," he said. "And if nobody gave him any money he would probably be forced into a training program that would teach him some trade and maybe he would make a better living for himself. And then, again, maybe that's all wrong."

And that was the last he said about that. That's when I figured the guy must have been just a little touched. When I thought about it later there were some ways he could have been right about the blind guy, but I still didn't see any connection between that and my allowance. When I thought about Chris, I still didn't think he was guilty. But then I hadn't known about the money. Chris was a standoffish kind of guy, and even though we were all pulling for him we weren't that close to him. So we invited him over to the renting office more than we had in the past, and he started coming over. He seemed really glad to have someone on his side.

"You know how I felt when they arrested me?" he said. "I felt guilty."

"Well, you're not guilty and that's all that counts," I said.

"I wish the trial was tomorrow, though," he said. "Until they find me not guilty everyone's still going to think I am."

"Suppose they find you guilty," Bubba said.

"How can they find him guilty when he's not?" Dean spoke up. "If you're not guilty you're not guilty."

"That's not true, man," Bubba said, burying his hand wrist-deep in Gloria's almost empty potato chip bag to get the crumbs. "It don't matter if you guilty or innocent. The only thing that matters is if the jury believes you guilty or innocent. Now, take this cat I read about. They put him on trial for killing his wife and they hung his butt. Then about four years later they found another cat who killed about nine people, and he said, 'Oh, yeah, remember that guy who you hung for killing his wife? Well, I was the one that really did it.' But it was too late then, because they hung the dude."

"That's a big help, Bubba," Gloria said. "You got any more good-doing messages of inspiration?"

"I'm just warning Chris that he might have to go to jail even if he is innocent," Bubba said, licking his fingertips and then running them along the inside crease of the potato chip bag to get the real small crumbs. "So it won't be no shock or nothing."

"That's what I'm afraid of, really," Chris said. "Sometimes it almost seems as if I am guilty."

"We're kind of looking around to see if we come up with any clues," Gloria said. "If we do we'll tell the police."

"You got a lawyer?" I asked.

"Yeah, a woman from Legal Aid."

"You got a woman lawyer?" Gloria asked.

"Yeah."

"Can I ask you a question?" I asked.

"Go ahead." Chris looked at me.

"My father said you were spending a lot of money."

"Yeah?"

"That's it." I shrugged, not wanting to ask the next question. I didn't have to, Bubba did it for me.

"We thought there wasn't no money taken," Bubba said.

"Thanks," Chris said, standing. "It's really cool having friends in your corner."

To say that our discussion with Chris had gone over like a lead balloon would be the understatement of the year. But one thing still bothered me. He might have been disap-

108

pointed in us for asking about the money and all, but where did he get it?

A. B. Tucker, Bubba reported, had been interested in us buying some hi-fi equipment, but he wanted to see our money. What we didn't have, any of us, was money. Gloria's idea about the street fair was really good, I thought, but it would take a while to get it organized, and we needed some money right away. It was getting near the end of the month, and we thought we might collect some of the rents (for a change) and use some of that money to show A. B. so we could see what equipment he would turn up with. We went to Pender.

"Oh, no," Mr. Pender said. "One doesn't rob Peter to pay Paul, even if it is to save Paul who has been accused of robbing Peter!"

"Right, whatever you said," Dean said. "Does that mean we can't get no dust?"

"It means that if you're really serious about bringing the building into some sort of financial health you can't start taking money out of the operating funds for other purposes."

"What's an operating fund?" Bubba asked.

"The money you use to pay your bills and keep the building in repair," Mr. Pender said.

That all seemed right, and we just sat around for a while as Mr. Pender showed us the books and how different items were being paid up. It looked as if we might be even in another nine months, he said. He had applied for the forms for tax relief for buildings which were being repaired, and that could help. It didn't help to get the money for A. B., and I realized that we were losing some of our enthusiasm in helping Chris and in keeping the building going, just because it was so hard.

"You got any ideas?" Dean asked Mr. Pender.

"When I was a young man struggling to be a poet—"

"You were going to be a poet?" Bubba asked.

"There is nothing so unrecognizable as a faded dream," Mr. Pender said. "Yes, I was going to be a poet. When I was going through that particular phase of my life, there were often times when I or one of my colleagues was unable to meet the obligations of our dwelling. Heaven often sent the Muse, but never the rent. At any rate, when those times came we would have rent parties. We would charge a dollar to get in, and we'd sell food and what have you. Everyone would have a fine time at the party, and we would raise enough money to pay the rent."

That's how our rent party began. At first we were going to have it in the office, but then Gloria came up with the idea of having it in Mr. Hyatt's apartment. This was a good idea, and Dean and Gloria went to see Mr. Hyatt at the hospital and ask him. Bubba wanted to go, too, but we didn't let him. He'd probably start telling Mr. Hyatt about how he knew some guy who had died in the same bed he was laying in or something. Mr. Hyatt okayed the party and was really kind of glad that we were having it in his apartment. He told us to have a drink for him, which was supposed to be funny, I guess, but wasn't really, because he still wasn't doing too good.

We sent invitations to everyone in the building, and Tina

110

Robinson agreed to be the hostess. We also went around the neighborhood and invited people we knew and asked if anybody wanted to donate anything. Most people didn't want to donate anything, but Chippy's, a fish-and-chip place near the corner, promised to give us twenty-five dollars' worth of fish and chips.

The party started out quietly, and a lot of people came, so it looked as if everything was going to work out. Then the screaming started and the party got out of hand. Mrs. Brown from the top floor was one of the first people to get to the party. She asked if she could help, and we said that we had everything pretty much under control, but she insisted. So Gloria decided that she would be clever, and she asked Mrs. Brown if she would keep track of how many people actually came to the party. This seemed like a good idea, and we settled Mrs. Brown in a chair near the door, and she marked off a stroke for everyone that came in. I got her some punch and she really seemed happy, watching everybody standing around or dancing. She also said that Mr. Johnson wasn't feeling well and that perhaps he would be down later, and that if he did he would be the hit of the party because everyone liked to have boxers at parties, especially when they were the champions of the world.

Mr. Pender had told us a few things about Jack Johnson. He said that he had been the first black heavyweight champion way back before the first World War. He had been a hero to many black people the same way that Muhammad Ali was a hero. It was funny, because none of us had ever heard of him or thought about people like Mrs. Brown having their own heroes.

"Mrs. Brown must have been a little girl when he was champion," he said. "And she's kept his memory alive long after he died. We all keep our delusions with us. Sometimes it's a person, sometimes an idea, sometimes even a dream that seems more real in memory than it ever did in life. Jack Johnson was the champion of the world. Not a bad choice," he said, "not a bad choice at all."

The party was going pretty good, and Tina was talking about having a dance contest just to liven things up in the middle. Now Tina was answering the door if Gloria or me weren't near. Whoever answered the door would say something like "Welcome to the party," and then run into a quick explanation of why we were having the party. Some people weren't interested, but some were, and they kind of dug the idea of having a good time and doing some good at the same time. When the Captain came to the door no one was around to answer it except Mrs. Brown, and she told him to come right on in and enjoy himself. Then she asked him if he was a prizefighter, and he didn't say nothing, he just looked at her kind of funny.

"If you need a job, you can always come around to Mr. Johnson—that's Mr. Jack Johnson, the champion of the world—he can always use young men for sparring partners."

The way she said this, sort of like a queen, waving her hand in the air and everything, was really cool.

The Captain still didn't say nothing, just looked at her for a minute, and then came on in and sat down. So far, so good.

The party was still going on when there was another

knock on the door. I started toward the door, then I saw that Mrs. Brown was going to get there before me, so I started back to the kitchen where Tina and Gloria and another girl I didn't know were making little sandwiches. That's when the screaming started.

The first scream scared me half to death. I ran into the other room, and I saw that Mrs. Brown had passed out. I started over toward her when I heard the second scream. This time it was Gladys, Mr. Gilfond's wife, from the first floor. I looked up, and she had her hand over her mouth and was pointing toward the door with the other hand. I looked to where she was pointing and saw what the screaming was all about.

Askia Ben Kenobi was standing in the doorway dressed in a turban, some little gold shorts, and a cape. That's it. Honest. He looked like some dude from the Arabian Nights or some fairytale book.

"Man, what is you doing?" The Captain looked at Askia.

"I am being me," Askia said in this real spooky voice.

"Where your clothes, sucker?" the Captain said.

"I am clothed in purity," Askia said. He was standing really tall and looking around the room real slow. "For the essence of the black man is purity."

"You better get your butt out of here and put some clothes on!" Tina said, coming out of the kitchen.

"And what you got smeared all over yourself?" the Captain asked. "Crisco?"

"It is sacred palm oil," Askia said, bowing.

Askia Ben Kenobi was covered with something that made him shiny. It looked like that oil that body builders put on themselves, or it could have been Crisco.

"I don't care what kind of lard you got on yourself, you better go someplace with your dumb self!" Tina was yelling. She was really mad. I didn't think she could get that mad. In fact, when she lifted the plate of cheese dip over her head I still didn't believe she was going to throw it. She threw it. It went right at Askia Ben Kenobi.

But Askia Ben Kenobi was good. I mean really good. The cheese dip came at him about waist high, and he kicked it away with one of his karate kicks.

Tina wasn't giving up that easy, and she threw a handful of the little sandwiches we had made at him, and he knocked them away, too. This time he used his hands. You could hardly see him move, he was so fast. *Whack! Whack! Whack!* And the sandwiches were all over the room. I don't know who threw the sparerib bone, but it caught him right behind the left ear. He whirled and made a step in that direction, and then everybody started throwing things at him. Spareribs, handfuls of cheese dip, and roasted peanuts. The fish and chips hadn't arrived yet.

He fought some of them off, but you could see it was a losing battle. And, although none of the stuff was hurting him, the cheese dip was sticking to the grease he had on, and after a while he looked really grimy. Then he sort of pulled his cape around himself and tried to stare everybody down, but that didn't work either because it was really fun throwing stuff at him. I knew we'd have to clean it up later, but that was later—right now the cheese dip was flying. A guy with a gold tooth who was a friend of Tina's got too close to Askia, and Askia gave him a karate kick in the stomach. The guy doubled up with pain. Things turned from funny to really serious just like that! I remembered the banister that Askia Kenobi had torn up, and I backed away a few steps. The Captain jumped up from where he was sitting and tried to grab Askia, but every time he grabbed something Askia just slipped away. It was like trying to grab a greased pig. Only, when he would slip away he would throw a few karate punches. The Captain was bleeding from the nose. He was on one side of the room and Askia was on the other. The Captain started rushing across the floor with his short fat legs going about a mile a minute, and Askia started from his side. This time it was the Captain who slipped and went down, and Askia flew over him onto a card table where they had been playing Tonk. The card table collapsed, and Gladys Gilfond, who was still holding her hand from before the whole thing with Askia started, fell across him.

That's when they finally got Askia down. He struggled a little more, but he had hurt his foot pretty bad, so it was just about over. The Captain called a friend of his who was a cop, and he and another cop came and took Askia away in handcuffs. I found out later they just made him walk around the block and then took him up to his apartment again.

By the time we had gotten Mrs. Brown calmed down and the place cleaned up, the party was over. Mr. Pender reached the party at eleven-thirty, just as the last people were leaving. We did a quick tally and saw that we had actually made money, though. To be exact, we had made four dollars and thirty cents.

# CHAPTER
## 12

"YOU SEE, YOU ARE FOLLOWING WHAT I CALL THE LINE OF the people who watch history." A. B. Tucker tilted his head all the way back, and the soda he was drinking went down in two large gulps. "I am of those who make history. Dig, you know I am what is commonly called a thief, is that correct?"

"Yeah," Bubba said.

"Okay, and you think that stealing is wrong," A. B. said. "Is that also correct?"

"That's right," Gloria said. "And there's nothing you can tell me that's going to make me change my mind, either."

"Okay, what you got to tell me about Sam, then?"

"Who's Sam?" I asked, knowing that was what I was supposed to ask.

"Sam is this cat that lives on Park Avenue, near the White Rose Bar. One day Sam went over to one of them furniture stores—you know the kind, you get three rooms of furniture for two hundred dollars plus they throws in a television set?"

"Yeah, go on."

"Well, he goes over there and they charge my man two hundred and one dollars for this living room set, see. And then he gets his old lady to go downtown when they deliver it, and he's all happy and smiling. Now, when they deliver the stuff and his old lady comes in and sees it, she's all smiling and everything because she's happy. Sam, he goes over and puts on the television and they go to sit on the couch and *blam!* the couch falls down. He looks at the couch and he sees that there's marbles and stuff on the inside of the couch. A pocket comb is in there and right away he knows it ain't new stuff. So he goes over to the store and tells the man and the man says that he never did say it was new stuff. So Sam says he don't want this stuff and the man says he don't blame him, but there's nothing he can do about it because he's done sold the contract to another guy. Sam is mad. But Sam is also a little what they call peculiar. He says that because the guy got a store he got to steal a little bit or he wouldn't make no living, see? But Sam, he got him a limit on how much you can steal from him. His limit is two hundred dollars. You remember how much I told you that set cost?"

"Two hundred and one dollars," I said.

"Right on! So Sam tells the man to give him back a dollar, and the man says he ain't gonna do no such a thing. So Sam lays for the cat outside and puts a knife up against the man's throat and takes back his dollar so that he keep his limit. What happened after that was Sam got put in jail for stealing a dollar from the man. The man done stole two hundred dollars from Sam and everybody says that's all right, see? So when I steal, I'm just looking at things from the way the man in the store looks at it and the way the law looks at it. Which is, there ain't nothing wrong with stealing, just don't get caught breaking no laws when you do it. Sam broke the law that says you can't be putting no knife up against a man's throat and taking his dollar. There ain't no law that says you can't steal from a man if he's just stupider than you."

"That's some messed-up logic," Gloria said.

"That's the same thing that Sam said when they took him off to jail," A. B. said. "You some kin to Sam?"

"No," Gloria said. "But it's still some messed-up logic. You just want us to believe that stealing is right."

"No, I'm just telling you that you would have invited that dude that ran the store to your little party last night but you didn't invite me," A. B. said. "You probably made a whole lot of money and was afraid I was going to try to steal it or something. But in all my life I have never stole nothing from a friend."

"Well, we did make a little money," I said, nudging Gloria. "At least a couple of dollars."

"At least," Gloria said, smiling as if she knew something.

"I heard you made a lot of money," A. B. said. "I also heard you had a big fight. When there's a lot of money floating around a party, people fight in a minute. There's only two things people fight over—women and money—and

I didn't hear nobody talking about how many women you had there."

Gloria and I kept on acting like we were in on something, and A. B. told us that we should come on over to this place he knew and maybe we could see some really dynamite stereo equipment. We said we would think about it, but we weren't too anxious. A. B. said to think about it real hard because he would be around later that night and take one of us over to the place if we wanted to go.

When A. B. left we were really happy. We didn't have any money, but we were still going to see the stuff and maybe find some of the stuff that was stolen from Mr. Reynolds' store.

Chris came by a little later and said how he was sorry about being upset when we questioned him about the money. Then we said we were sorry for questioning it. He told us that Mr. Reynolds had given him his vacation pay and told him that he would try to believe in him until he was proved guilty or not guilty. That really seemed decent of Mr. Reynolds, and I felt a little worse about questioning where Chris had got the money from. Chris said that he told Mr. Reynolds how we were trying to help him, and he said that it was good but that we should be careful.

We met A. B. the next evening. He came with another guy who he said was his driver. The guy had a car, one of those gypsy cabs, and we got into it. Me and Gloria sat in the back, and A. B. and the driver sat in the front. We drove downtown for a while, and then we started back uptown. But when we started uptown, A. B. pulled down some curtains that covered the windows and a curtain that went along the back of the front seat so we couldn't see where we were going.

"They the curtains of joy," A. B. said, "in case my man got to drive some lovebirds around, or something like that."

When we got to where we were going, we went in the back way. The only thing we could see was that we were in a backyard. I thought I heard a train pass by. It sounded like the el train. Later, when we left, it was by the same way.

The warehouse was dirty and dingy on the outside but really nice and clean on the inside. You had to walk up the stairs because the elevator didn't work. Gloria went with me, and she took my hand once we got inside. I couldn't think for a moment when she took my hand. My mind just went blank, and I looked at her and smiled and she smiled back. I was definitely going to have to do something about Gloria.

One half of the floor we stopped on had dresses and coats, rows and rows of dresses and then rows and rows of coats. It was the most stuff I had ever seen that wasn't in a store.

"This is all hot stuff?" Gloria asked.

"That's right," A. B. said.

There were some other guys there, too. Some were just hanging around and some were showing stuff to the guy who acted as if he was running the place. Then there were some girls who answered the phones.

On the other side of the floor there was all kinds of radio and television equipment. They were in two sections, an A section and a B section. Each carton was marked with an A or a B, depending on what section it was in.

"The stuff in the A section has warranty papers," A. B.

said. "That's good stuff and you can sell it anywhere. The stuff on the B side is the same kind of stuff, but it don't have warranty papers, so you can only sell it to people. You can't sell it to stores or nothing like that. Now, you just look around to see what you want. The stuff on the A side is a hundred dollars. Anything you want is a hundred dollars. The side without the warranties is fifty dollars. Anything you want over there you get for fifty dollars."

We thought it would be cool to see what A. B. Tucker had. All we would have to do is to spot the stuff from Mr. Reynolds' store, report it to the police, and Chris would be cleared. Well, it didn't work that way. We didn't know where the warehouse was, to begin with. Next, Gloria had some bad news.

"Did you see that dude standing near the door?" she asked when A. B. had let us out of the car near Riverside Drive. "The dark dude with the skullcap?"

"Yeah, I saw him," I said. "So what?"

"He had a gun sticking out of his back pocket," she said. "A real gun?"

A real gun. I didn't have to ask. Gloria just looked at me and I looked at her, and suddenly the idea of Chris going to jail didn't seem so bad. I didn't even think about the reward money. I knew that wasn't right, to fink out on a friend just because you were a little scared. I said this to Gloria, about how it wasn't the most honorable thing in the world.

"I know what you mean, though," she said.

We got back to The Joint, and Bubba and Dean were there, playing checkers. They asked us how it went, and we told them what had happened.

"All we got to do is to tell the police," Bubba said. "Then they can get A. B. and make him tell them where the warehouse is, see. Then the police can go through the stuff and check out what belongs to Mr. Reynolds and what don't."

"Suppose they can't make him tell?" Gloria asked. "And the guy with the gun gets arrested. What are you going to say then?"

"I'm going to say the same thing I'm saying now," Bubba said. "You either got the guts to do what's right or you ain't."

I really wished that Bubba hadn't put it like that, because I wasn't sure if I had the guts to do what was right or not. Then Dean had to stick his two cents in.

"Suppose A. B. didn't steal that stuff," Dean said.

"It's still stolen stuff," Bubba said.

"Yeah, but suppose A. B. didn't steal it?"

"So?"

"Well, if A. B. didn't steal it, if he's just selling it, suppose some other guys did it?"

"If A. B. didn't steal it, then some other guys had to steal it," I said.

"Right." Dean was nodding his head. "Remember that gang that stole that money, about five million dollars, from the airport?"

"Yeah?"

"And remember how they kept finding bodies all the time?"

"They didn't steal this stuff," Bubba said.

"But suppose someone *like* them stole the stuff," Dean said, "and the stuff they said Chris took wasn't even there.

Then they would be mad at us and we wouldn't have solved anything."

"We could use a little more evidence," Bubba said. "We really don't know that stuff was even stolen stuff, really."

"It was stolen," I said.

"Would you swear to God on a stack of Bibles facing your mother's grave?" Bubba asked.

"My mother isn't dead," I said.

"Would you swear in court knowing all those guys are on the loose with a stack of bullets?" Dean said. "If we're going to be heroes, we'd at least better get some good evidence."

"What do you say, Bubba?" I asked. "You're the one with the guts."

"Maybe we'll wait until we find out for sure where the place is," Bubba said.

The idea didn't sound like it would look good on paper, but it sure felt good. We had found a new way to spell relief: C-H-I-C-K-E-N!

# CHAPTER
## 13

WHEN I WENT TO BED I DIDN'T GET TO SLEEP EASILY, BUT I must have drifted off because the next thing I remember is waking up with a lot of commotion going on in the kitchen. It was the middle of the night and at first I just ignored it, but then I went out to see what was going on. My father was sitting at the table, and he was really upset, and there was a telegram. I looked at my mother.

"Your uncle passed away," she said.

Early the next morning there was a lot of confusion in the house. My mother was getting ready to go to work, and my father was getting ready to go to West Virginia where his brother had lived. Mom asked me if I would go with him. I didn't know my uncle, but how could I say no? If somebody dies you're supposed to feel sorry for them even if you don't like them, or at least if you didn't like them when they were living, you were supposed to say it was okay now that they were dead. So I went with my father. He didn't say much on the way to the airport. I tried talking to him once in a while, but I didn't make a big thing of it.

We took the shuttle from New York to Washington and then rented a car and drove to Martinsburg, West Virginia. It had started raining, and one of the windshield wipers, the one on my side, wasn't working too well. I imagined the water to be a map of first one country and then another as the wiper changed the patterns on the window.

"One time"—my father's voice was hoarse as he spoke—"your uncle and me went down to the veterans' hospital on a Saturday night. We didn't have anything in mind, really— we just wandered down there. A door was open and we went in and walked down the hall until we came to an office. There was a metal box on the desk in the office. Jerry opened it and we saw that it was a money box. There wasn't a lot of money in it, maybe twenty dollars or so, not enough to amount to much now, but it was a lot then."

My father stopped talking again and continued driving. We went along a fairly wide highway for a while and then turned off onto a smaller road. The houses along the side of the road were neat but small and stood just off the edge of the road as if they were waiting for something that might never come.

"What happened then?" I asked.

"Then?" My father took a quick look at me. "Well, we hadn't had what you would call a planned meal for over a week. My father had gone over to Harrisburg looking for work and we hadn't heard from him. To make a long story short, we took the money. We didn't say anything to each other, we just took the money. He took some first and then I took some. We went out into the hall and found that the door that we had come in was locked. Somebody had left it open while they went out for something, but you had to have a key to get out. We went down the hall toward the front of the hospital. We saw a door that was open and we started toward it when we heard somebody yell out. I turned and saw the guard coming toward us. Jerry ran back down the hall toward the guard, and the guard grabbed him and I ran out the door.

"I got home that night and waited for Jerry to come home and he didn't. The next morning the sheriff came around and said that he was caught in the hospital stealing money. He told them he had been with a boy he had just met, and I never got into trouble."

"Did he get into trouble?"

"Not much," my father said. "He got two months' probation. Right after that, though, he quit school, started hanging around and drinking. Never amounted to much, really."

"How come," I asked, "if he really didn't get into any trouble?"

"Guess he was just looking for an excuse to give up," my father said, "and we found one that night."

When we got to Martinsburg we went through the center of town to a place where there was a group of houses, gray and huddled, near what looked like it had once been a freight yard. You could still see tracks showing through in some places where the paved streets had worn down. Some of the houses were patched with tar paper, especially near the windows. We stopped at one of the places. Everybody said hello to my father, and some of the women started crying as soon as they saw him. They asked if I was his boy, and he said yes, and they said things about how I looked like him and that kind of thing. They were black, the same as me, but they were like country people.

"I was born and raised here," my father said to me. That was all he said to me in the five hours or so we were there. We went with other cars to the church, taking some of the people with us in the rented car. I guess my father knew there wouldn't be enough cars to take all the people, which was why he had rented the car in Washington. The funeral was quiet, with not too much preaching or anything—even the crying was quiet, and I felt almost as if they were trying to keep the rest of the world from knowing that one of them had died. Afterwards we ate and sat around for a while, and then my father said we had to leave.

"Y'all take care of yourselves," one woman said. She was thin, and her wrists looked as if they would break if you grabbed them too tightly. She was my Uncle Jerry's wife. She came up to my father, and they held each other for a while, and then we left. When we got into the car and my father had started it up, I began to turn around to see them one last time.

"Don't look back," my father said harshly.

But I already had, and they were standing there looking at

us getting ready to leave, and they didn't look a whole lot different than the stones in the graveyard as they stood together in the last light of the day.

We drove back to Washington and left the car. I felt glad when we got on the plane and were headed back to New York. All the way back home I thought about my father living there and being with those people. It was a part of his life that I hadn't even suspected was there, and I wondered how much more there was to him.

"Do you feel bad about your brother?" I asked. "I mean about what happened after he stole the money?"

"Yeah," he said, folding his hands, "I do."

"It wasn't your fault that he drank or anything," I said.

"I know," my father said. "It wasn't my fault that things went wrong, and I guess it's not my fault that I couldn't think of anything to do for him after things did go wrong. But I lost Jerry somewhere—long before he died, I lost him."

"I guess it's a funny feeling," I said, "kind of like a person dying even before they're dead."

He nodded, and then we stopped talking. It was early in the morning when we got back home. He came in to say good night after I got in bed. I wondered, as I lay in bed kind of sorting things out, if he thought I might not make a go of it, like his brother, and that he might lose me, too. Losing people like that, the way my father put it, was scary. I thought about who I might lose, and then I thought that maybe I didn't have anybody to lose because nobody was my responsibility, and I wasn't that close to anybody except my parents, and I didn't figure to lose them. Gloria could lose people easier than me, I thought, because she got closer to people than I did. I didn't know if that was good or bad, and I really didn't want to think about it too much, because I didn't have any real answers.

# CHAPTER
## 14

WHEN I GOT UP LATER THAT MORNING MY FATHER HAD already gone to work. I went down to The Joint and saw a crowd gathered in front of the building. I tried to figure out what was happening from the faces in the crowd, but I couldn't. All I could see was Tina standing on the top step and screeching her head off.

"He's going to kill us all!" she was shouting. "We all going to be dead any minute now!"

"Who's down there?" I asked, not wanting to really know. I was hoping she didn't say Bubba's body or something like that.

"That Petey, that's who!" Tina said. "He's got a still down there, and he's going to blow us all sky-high one of these days. I called the police and they're going to be here any minute!"

"You oughta mind your business, you old four-eyed witch!" a woman called out from the sidewalk.

I didn't understand what was going on, and I asked Tina to run the whole thing by me one more time.

"Petey got a still in the basement," she said, out of breath for some reason. "And them things blow in a minute! We could all be killed!"

I went down to the basement, and the door was locked. I banged on it and called Mr. Darden. He came to the door after a while and asked who it was, and I told him it was me. He let me in and I asked him what was going on.

"That skinny little wench done gone and called the police because I'm mixing up a little brew here in the basement," he said.

"She said you got a still," I said.

"Ain't nothing but a little brew," Mr. Darden said.

"Can it blow up?"

"If it does it'll be her fault," he said. "I'm supposed to be supplying the brew for this party down the street, and I had to turn the fire up full blast just to get it out so I can get things cleaned up before the police get here."

"Mr. Darden," I said, remembering that he had brought some kind of liquor to the rent party we gave, "are you kidding me?"

"No," he answered. "I ain't kidding and there's not one little thing to worry about except what the police gonna say when they get here and find there ain't nothing here. Because as soon as this mess is finished cooking, I'm gonna tear the whole thing down and put it away so fast you won't even know it was here."

The next thing I knew Bubba was coming down the stairs asking how come there were police cars stopping in front of the place. I didn't know what to say, but I ran upstairs anyway and saw that there were two cars stopped outside of the place. One of the cars was across the street and the other right in front. The crowd was moving around in front of The Joint, and Tina was still standing outside of the door on the stoop. Right then I had a bright idea.

"Tina," I called to her, "quick, go up to your apartment so the cops will find you home!"

She looked at me kind of funny and took one little step back.

"Go ahead," I said, motioning with my hands, "quick."

Tina gave me another look, like she was puzzled, and took another backward step. I motioned with my hands again and she went inside. She didn't know what I was up to, but she was just going along. By then two of the cops had come up and I was just about to tell them that Tina was upstairs, which I thought would give me more time to convince Mr. Darden to take the still down, when—*WHOOOSH!*—a big sound came from the basement.

Everybody that was in front of the building started running this way and that, and the cops backed off in a hurry. I heard one of them yell for somebody to call the bomb squad. I ran into the building and down the back stairs toward the other entrance to the basement. I opened the door, and there was the worst smell I had ever smelled in my life. Mr. Darden opened the door to where the boiler room was,

132

and the floor was covered with slime and mess. There was a small fire, and Mrs. Darden was trying to stamp it out with her foot, only she was slipping around in the mess from the still so much she couldn't get it out. There was a bucket of sand standing near the wall, and Mr. Darden came and got that and threw it on the fire and put it out.

"Don't you worry none," he said, snatching down some of the pipes, which must have been really hot because he would snatch at one and then jerk his hand back. "I'm going to have this whole thing cleared up in two shakes. Just you wait and see."

I waited and what I saw was Mr. and Mrs. Darden trying to sweep up the mess. It smelled awful, and it was slippery, and I just hoped it wouldn't catch on fire again.

When I got upstairs, the police had cleared the street, and a truck marked 532nd Bomb Disposal Squadron was there. Two guys came out and were talking to the cops. They had a loudspeaker and were trying to get the building evacuated.

"I think everything's cleared up now," I said to one of the cops.

"Who lives down there?" he asked. "Arabs?"

"Yeah," I said, knowing that Mr. Darden was from Georgia, and that seemed to do him a lot of good.

You know who got in trouble after all that? Not Mr. Darden, because he said he didn't have a still in the basement. He said he was sleeping and he heard a loud noise. Me. I got a summons for having a building violation. I didn't even believe it. But that's what happened. The cops and the bomb squad left, and people started gathering around and asking Mr. Darden if he really had a still in the basement, and he just looked like he was being too modest to say anything about it. A couple of people said that if he ever got it going again they would order from him.

Tina came down to the office and told me that either Petey Darden had to go or she would go.

"Tina," I said, "I don't really care. If you go, then we'll have an empty apartment on one floor. If Mr. Darden goes we'll have an empty apartment on another floor. What can I tell you?"

"Well," she said, putting her hand on her hip, "I can tell you one thing. I'm not going!"

Gloria came over and I told her the whole story. We were sitting around talking about it and just sort of goofing around in general when Mrs. Brown came down and said that, in all the excitement, Jack Johnson had had a heart attack and died. She was crying so badly that we thought about calling the doctor. She said that she couldn't go up to the apartment alone, and Gloria said that she understood, that she would go with her.

I sent Jackie, a little girl that hung around the office sometimes, out for two containers of coffee. I had begun to drink a lot of coffee, and I was beginning to feel old. I looked at the calendar. There were still five weeks before school started.

Gloria stayed with Mrs. Brown almost two hours. Dean came by and we talked about nothing in particular. When Gloria came down, I asked her how Mrs. Brown was doing, and she said okay, that she would go and check on her after a while.

"You know, I really think you're okay," I said to Gloria. "I really mean it."

"Really mean that I'm okay?" Gloria asked.

"I guess so," I said, chickening out. I wanted to say something else to her, but I lost the nerve, or maybe the right words, somewhere along the way.

"If you mean that I care for people, you're right," Gloria said. "Is that what you mean?"

"I guess so," I said.

"We still going to work on finding out who stole the stuff from Mr. Reynolds' store?" she asked.

I nodded.

"Is that really what you meant?" Gloria asked. "About me being okay? Just that I care for people?"

I was embarrassed and I smiled, and she smiled, too, and I felt about ten feet high. Gloria had a way of doing that to me.

# CHAPTER
## 15

WE WERE IN THE JOINT WHEN A FRIEND OF GLORIA'S CAME
in and said that her mother had said that we were in the
newspaper. So we went out and got a *Daily News* and a
*Times* and the *Amsterdam News,* but we couldn't find a
word. Gloria called her mother, but her mother didn't know
what paper we were in either. It seems a friend of Gloria's
from school had called her house and said that she had read
something about us in the paper. Gloria's mother had told a
friend, who came and told us. So we called the girl who had
called her mother, and she wasn't home. We were about to
forget about it when the girl—her name was Karen—
showed up.

"Gloria!"

"Hey, what are you doing over here?" Gloria gave Karen five and they went through their little number about giving each other five and bumping hips and what have you. They looked cute doing it, too. Only, by this time, I have to admit, Gloria was getting cuter every day and whatever she did I liked. She had my nose open, so to speak.

"Is this the place you're messing with?" Karen asked.

"Yeah," Gloria said. "Look, everybody, this is my friend Karen, and these are my friends Paul, Dean, and Bubba."

Karen smiled at everybody, and everybody sort of nodded at her.

"Who's Paul Williams?" Karen asked, checking the paper she was carrying for the name.

"I am," I said.

"You look like a slumlord," she said.

Well, the whole bit was this. *The Village Voice* was doing an article on slumlords in the city, and they had my name listed as the owner of The Joint. Really. I looked at the paper, and there, big as day, was my name. Not only that, but next to my name it said, "Possible mob connections."

Gloria tried to explain to Karen how I really wasn't a slumlord, but she didn't sound too convincing.

I was getting a little uptight about the whole thing, too. Nobody seemed to want to know about the problems with the building, but everybody wanted a little piece of the criticism. From wanting to make a go of The Joint, I had come around to just wanting to get people off my back. I wondered if Harley saw the article. He was probably laughing his head off if he did.

We decided to send a letter to *The Voice*. At first we were going to make it a real angry letter, saying how we were being picked on and everything. But then we figured that they probably wouldn't believe us anyway. Dean said that even if they did believe us, they couldn't print our letter because it would make them look bad. He had a point. So we decided on a letter that said how much we were going to improve the building. Which was a little bit of a joke because we didn't have any money.

"If we did take the money that Chris's father's boss put up for a reward," Gloria said, "we could do something. At least we'd have a few dollars."

It was a short-term solution, and it didn't look like it would make much difference in the long run, but it was all we had. We agreed to do it. We didn't have any idea if we could actually help out in the case or not, but it was worth a try. We decided to try to follow A. B. Tucker. That way we could find out where the warehouse was. The tail was a toss-up between Dean and Bubba, because A. B. had gone with me and Gloria to the warehouse. If he saw Dean or Bubba, maybe he wouldn't figure them to be tailing him. Anyway, we had Bubba and Dean draw straws. Bubba was elected to tail A. B. Tucker, but then it was decided that Dean should do the tailing because he had a bike and A. B. didn't know him as well as he did the rest of us.

We also knew that we were going to have to get a list of the stolen stuff from Mr. Reynolds, and Bubba was sent to do that. Finally, our money crisis was getting worse. The rent party had been a disaster, and the idea of having another one, as suggested by Mr. Pender, didn't hit anyone right. We had only five tenants who were paying their rent on a regular basis. Mr. Lowe and Mrs. Brown on the top floor paid each month on time. He worked in the post office and she collected Social Security and a small pension. Tina and Johnnie Mae Robinson paid. They were the only ones on the second floor. Mr. Hyatt usually paid okay when he wasn't in the hospital, but he was in there now. Ella Fox had always had trouble paying. On the first floor the Gilfonds paid, and so did Mrs. Jones. She worked in the St. James Hotel on 45th Street as a chambermaid. Mr. Darden and his wife lived in the basement and did the cleaning and odd jobs instead of paying rent. Of the nonpayers, the worst was Askia Ben Kenobi on the third floor. I didn't know how *The Voice* expected me not to be a slumlord if some people didn't pay their rent.

Mr. Pender said that we had enough money to last for three more weeks before we went bust. That's with all the payers paying. He showed me his figures, and they looked reasonable. One thing I noticed was that there was no mention of his salary. He hadn't collected a penny for keeping the books, and even though he was just doing it part time, I felt bad.

The thing was, really, that I had given up. If someone had come along and said, "Hey, here's a good excuse," I'd have grabbed it so fast it would have made your head spin. Gloria wanted to keep on going, but I didn't. Bubba wasn't really that interested, and Dean was just beginning to pick up a little in his interest. It seemed that everything that happened had the effect of stopping the rent. The Gilfonds, for example, broke up for about two days, and the rent was a week late because he went out and lost the money somewhere. He came back two days after he had left, but he didn't have the money to pay the rent. When Mr. Pender asked him about it he jumped bad with Pender.

"You have to understand hostility," Pender said. "When people feel that their weaknesses are showing, their lack of education or finances or position, they become defensive. Somehow they think that if they're hostile enough you won't notice whatever it is they're lacking."

"What did you say to Gilfond?" I asked.

"I said peerio," Mr. Pender said brightly. "Chip, chip, peerio!"

"Oh."

The street fair idea was, more or less, our last hope of getting enough money to get through the following month. I told my father about it, and he came up with something I didn't know about. You could rent booths from the city for a nominal fee if you had an affair that promoted the city. So the street fair was named the I Love New York Street Fair. It was really encouraging to find out about the booths, because at least it seemed as if we were really going to be doing something for a change. We were going to have drawings, and people were going to sell food. Everyone that had something to sell or do could get a booth, and they, in turn, would give us some money to participate in the fair. Altogether thirty people, mostly people who had small stores, but some who didn't, wanted to participate. We decided to charge everyone twenty dollars, and nobody objected.

Mr. Pender had another idea. He said we should rent out the office. That way it would contribute another one hundred dollars a month to the income of The Joint. It was a good idea and one that we had to go along with, but we had gotten used to hanging out in the renting office and didn't really want to give it up. But we told Pender that we would get the furniture out of the office and rent it out right after the street fair.

Mr. Reynolds refused to give the list of stolen stuff to Bubba. He said that we shouldn't be fooling around in police business. We got a list of stuff from Chris, but he didn't know the serial numbers. Then someone—I think it was Gloria—got the idea of getting the numbers from the Police Department. As it turned out we didn't have to because Chris got the numbers from his attorney, the woman from Legal Aid. That made us feel good, because at least Chris seemed to be getting interested in the case. After all, it was his neck we were trying to save.

Dean had been trying to follow A. B. Tucker around for almost a week without results.

"Usually he gets into his car and takes off, and by the time I get my bicycle ready, he's gone," Dean said. "And when he's walking he just hangs around the same old places."

As luck would have it, though, it was me who found out where the warehouse was. I was going to a friend's house on La Salle Street, and who do I see but A. B. Tucker and this girl walking along Broadway. He was talking to her as if he was explaining something, and I watched him for a while from across the street. I was standing at the doughnut shop on 125th, and he was walking uptown on the other side. Now, the el train runs along Broadway, and I thought I'd heard a train the last time I went to the warehouse. I walked across the street from A. B. Tucker and the girl, staying as close as I could to the buildings so he wouldn't see me. I followed them for a while, and then I saw A. B. stop and go into a garage. At least it had "Garage" on the outside. He just opened the door and walked in. I could see that there was someone at the door when he walked in, but I couldn't see who it was. The girl didn't go in with him. She waited outside, and after a while A. B. came out. He had a box with him, and he and the girl hailed a cab. I was standing there watching him get into the cab, and then when the cab turned and went past me I looked the other way. I was sure he didn't see me, and I was pretty sure that the building he went in had to be the warehouse.

I was pretty excited by the time I got back to The Joint. I told Gloria, Bubba, and Dean what I had seen. They weren't exactly enthusiastic.

"So?" That was Dean.

"So?" I said, a little ticked that they didn't show more interest. "So now we know where the stolen stuff is!"

"No, we don't," Bubba said. "What we know is that there's some stuff in there that might be stolen. We don't know if the stuff from Mr. Reynolds' store is in there, and we don't know that the stuff that is in there is really even stolen."

"Not only that," Gloria said, "but I remember this picture where the hero found this warehouse where they were putting dope in cars to ship around the world, and he told the F.B.I. By the time the F.B.I. got to the warehouse it was empty."

"Hey, look, I don't get it," I said. "We've been planning to follow A. B. Tucker to find out where the warehouse is, and now we've done it and you guys don't even give a darn."

Gloria looked at Bubba and then at Dean.

"Me and Dean was over near the park," Bubba said, "and we saw Mr. Reynolds and we started talking to him, and then Dean said—"

"*I* said?" Dean jumped up. "*You* were the one that started talking about us having a clue!"

"Well, one of us said something about having a clue," Bubba said, giving Dean a dirty look.

"You tell him what the clue was?" I asked.

"We just said that the stuff might be in a warehouse someplace," Bubba said.

"And what did he say?"

"He just said that we should be careful," Dean said. "And then he said that sometimes guys get hurt when they try to handle things themselves, like in the newspaper this morning."

"What was in the newspaper this morning?" I asked.

Gloria had the morning paper and pushed it toward me. There was a story about a gang that had killed a witness out on Long Island.

"You guys aren't witnesses," I said.

"No, but we will be if we find out that the stuff is in the warehouse!" Bubba said.

"Well, I'm going to check it out," I said. "Maybe I'll go by there tonight."

No one else said anything. Gloria looked down at her hands. Bubba stuffed a cupcake into his mouth, and Dean looked at the ceiling. It wasn't what you would call a show of strength. We talked around a bit more without really saying anything, and then we split up. I kept trying to think about The Joint and the reward money.

My mother had stewed chicken that night. If there's anything I hate in the world, it's stewed chicken. My father asked me why I wasn't eating the chicken, and I told him I didn't like stewed chicken. I expected to hear his mouth—you know, the lecture about the starving children in India or China or wherever. Instead he came up with one of his little jokes. He's got these strange little jokes that he makes up and gets a big kick out of.

"You think you hate eating stewed chicken?" he said. "Well, just imagine how the chicken feels about it!"

Then he laughed. I didn't like that joke at all. In the first place, I don't like to think about animals being able to think. If you think that the animal can think, you have to come up with a long story to justify you eating the animal. So when my father makes a joke like that I don't think it's funny. He laughed, though. A little chuckle to himself.

"I think we got a new lead on Chris's case," I said.

"What does that mean?" he mumbled through a mouthful of rice and gravy.

"Maybe we can find the stuff that's stolen," I said.

"Suppose you find out that he's guilty," my father said. "Suppose you get a lead and check it out and find out that Chris stole the stuff. You going to turn your evidence over to the police?"

"He's not guilty!" I said.

"But if he is . . ."

"If he is, I'll turn it over to the police," I said.

144

"Well, that's good," he said.

He didn't say anything for a while, and I figured he was thinking about the case.

"You really want Chris to be guilty, don't you?" I asked.

"I don't want anyone to be guilty," he said. "But the truth of it is that somebody is."

What I had really wanted to get into was that I was a little scared about checking out the warehouse. I wanted to say something to him so he would be a little scared for me, or tell me that it was too dangerous, or something. But it didn't work out like that.

I fooled around with a crossword puzzle after supper. I say fooled around because I've never finished a crossword puzzle in my entire life. I was waiting until it got dark before I went to check out the warehouse. At least that's what I told myself. When it began to get dark, I wished I had gone when it was still light out.

I was just about to leave when the phone rang. My mother answered and it was Dean.

"Hello?"

"Hi, it's me," Dean said. "You still going to check out the warehouse?"

"Yeah."

"Darn it!"

"Does that mean you're going, too?"

"I guess so," Dean said, "but believe me, it's against my advice to myself!"

# CHAPTER
# 16

WE WENT BY THE JOINT TO PICK UP A FLASHLIGHT. GLORIA was there, and she said she would go with us. I told her that it might be better if she didn't, but when she said she wanted to, I was glad.

By the time we got to the place I thought was the warehouse, it was dark. Now, it gets dark everywhere at night. But this whole neighborhood gets darker than any place in the world. Really. It was so dark you couldn't even see the doors of the place. I remembered the guy that I saw standing near the door when A. B. Tucker went in. I told Gloria to go across the street and watch when Dean and me went in. I told her that if she heard any screaming to go get the cops on the double.

"And if you don't hear nothing, go get the cops on the double because they got us," Dean said.

"No, that means we're okay," I said. "But we'll be out in thirty minutes or less. After that, we're in trouble."

We left Gloria across the street and crossed under the el toward the warehouse. Dean asked me if I thought he was gay. It was a funny thing to ask at the time. I said no, and then he asked me if I minded holding his hand when we got inside. That was kind of funny. Later, I told myself, I would laugh.

We got to the door and walked right up to it and tried it. I figured that if there was somebody inside I could tell them some story about how I had gone to the wrong place or something. The door opened. We couldn't see a thing inside. I shined the flashlight inside the place. Nothing, but I thought it could be the place that A. B. Tucker took us to. So in we went. We closed the door and started toward where I thought the stairs were. They were there. We turned out the flashlight and went slowly up the stairs. Dean had his hand on my arm. I was never so glad to be touching any-body in my life as I was just then. We went up two flight of stairs and came to a door. I opened it slowly.

"Who's there!" A voice came from the darkness.

What we heard next sounded like either someone throw-ing a piece of rock or metal against the door or someone shooting at it. We started downstairs in the darkness. I dropped the flashlight and ran into Dean and we tumbled down the first flight, grabbing the best we could at the metal banister, until we hit the bottom.

"Who's there!" The voice from the top of the stairs.

"Shoot him!" That was Dean, and we heard a scuffling at the top of the steps as whoever it was was getting under cover.

We got up and got down the rest of the stairs as quickly as we could. By the time we hit the first floor we heard some barking behind us and we knew there were dogs in the place. Never mind. The barking was behind us, the front door was in front of us, and fear was in our feet. I got to the far wall first and couldn't find the door.

"You got a match?" I tried to whisper in the darkness.

"Who? Me?" Dean asked.

What a question! Who else? I groped around for the door. The dogs were coming closer, and I could see a light from the staircase we had just come down. A moment later I saw a flashlight.

"Shoot to kill!" Dean again.

The light disappeared. But I thought I saw the door. I went over to where I thought I saw it. Bingo.

"I got it!" I whispered as loudly as I could.

I heard Dean's footsteps coming toward me as I opened the door. I jumped out and Dean came right behind me. There was a loud bang and an echo. Someone had shot at us again. I ran across the street in a crouch, and I saw Dean doing the same thing.

"What's up?" Gloria saw us coming.

"Run!" I said. And the three of us ran down Broadway. I never knew Gloria could run that fast. Dean and me were probably tired from running down the stairs.

We got back to The Joint and we were so out of breath we couldn't even talk. Dean announced that he would see us in the morning and started for the door.

"Thanks for coming along," I said, "and thanks for thinking so fast when we were in there."

"Yeah," he said, "right. Look, if you want to check out anything else, let me know, so I can get out of town for the day."

Dean was okay. He was scared, the same as me, but he had gone, and he had thought fast when we were in the warehouse.

"What happened?" Gloria asked.

"We got shot at," I said.

"By who?" she asked, her breathing calming down a little.

"I don't know," I said, "but it sure was close."

We sat there for a while until our breathing was back to normal, and then we closed up the office.

Maybe it was the excitement—I don't know. It had to be something different. But when Gloria was standing there locking up the office and I was standing there next to her, it just came out. It was almost as if somebody else besides me said it.

"Gloria?"

"What?"

"I love you."

She started laughing.

I turned and walked out of the hallway. Behind me I could hear her calling me and still laughing. I turned around and she was leaning against the door, still laughing. I felt like change for two cents. I went on home. I washed up a little and went to bed. It was the first time in my life I had said that to a girl. It would also be the last. I couldn't fall asleep right away—in fact, I stayed up most of the night, just staring into the darkness.

I had a dream, not a real dream, but the kind of thing you have when you're half awake and half asleep. I was back in the warehouse, and the guy was coming down the stairs. I told Dean to head for the door as I distracted the guy with the gun. I had the flashlight and I went to one side and turned it on. I could see, out of the corner of my eye, Dean open and shut the door as the bullets slammed into the wall next to my head. I turned out the flashlight and moved into the middle of the floor and backed slowly toward the door. The guy didn't have a flashlight. I was safe. He fired a few more shots off in the darkness. How many had he fired? Five? Six? I reached behind me and found the doorknob and turned it slowly. I threw the flashlight across the darkened floor. He fired at the light as I opened the door. But somehow he spotted me silhouetted against the streetlight and fired once in my direction. I felt the bullet go into my chest and felt a burning sensation. I closed the door behind me and staggered across the street. Down the street, about a block away, I saw Dean running, passing the liquor store. Gloria was there. I reached out to her but fell before I could touch her hand. I looked up at her one last time before I died. She was sobbing. There, now she would be sorry.

Then I fell asleep.

When I woke the next morning the phone was ringing. I stumbled out into the kitchen and saw that my mother was out. What day was it? I looked at the calendar and saw that Wednesday hadn't been crossed out. Wednesday was my favorite day. I answered the phone and it was Gloria. I hung up. A moment later it started to ring again, but I ignored it and went to the bathroom.

I wandered down to The Joint and found Bubba sitting on the stoop. He was trying to balance two slices of pizza, one on each knee, and drink a Coke at the same time.

"You got some people in the office," he said, a big grin on his face.

"What kind of people?" I asked, trying to read something into his expression.

"Just the usual astral types," he said.

Okay. I went into the office and there, sitting cross-legged on the floor, was Askia Ben Kenobi and some girl. Now, Askia Ben Kenobi normally looks as weird as you want or need on a regular day. But the girl looked like something else. She had silver paint on her face, little stars on both cheeks and one on her chin. There was an eye painted right in the middle of her forehead, too.

"What can I do for you, Mr. Kenobi?" I asked, trying to get enough sarcasm into my voice to let him know that I was being sarcastic but not so much that he would get really ticked off.

"I am here to inform you that my queen has arrived." he said.

I figured out right away that he was talking about the weirdo sitting next to him.

"She can't move in with you unless you're married," I said, lying through my teeth. "It says so on the lease."

He started chanting. She started chanting, too. Being chanted at is kind of a different experience. I mean, you don't get chanted at every day. I remember whole months that have gone by and I wasn't even hummed at. Anyway, they started their chanting, him first and then her. That's the way they stopped, too. He stopped and then she stopped.

"Do you mind if we pray?" he asked.

"Go ahead," I said.

So they started praying. But the praying sounded a lot like the chanting. He was still cross-legged, only now he leaned all the way forward until his head touched the floor in front of him and he was kind of muttering and kind of humming. There weren't any words that I could just come out and call words that I knew. Maybe he was doing it in another language.

Anyway, they were doing it in front of the desk, and I was sitting at the desk, so it looked a little as if they were praying to me. That's what Mrs. Brown saw when she walked in.

"What are you people doing?" she said in a loud, high voice.

They didn't say anything, just kept on praying, or whatever it was they were doing.

"You must be disciples of the Devil!" Mrs. Brown's face looked furious. "Disciples of the Devil!"

When Askia and his lady had finished praying, he introduced her to me as Selassie Tafari and said she was from his people.

"I will," he said, "not need this!"

He handed me a paper. I looked at it and saw that it was an eviction notice. It must have been Pender's work. I looked up at Askia Ben Kenobi and saw that he had narrowed his eyes down to little slits.

I smiled a dumb little smile and sat down. Mrs. Brown

spit on the floor right in front of him, and he gave her a look, but she just gave him one right back and he left. The lady, Silver Face, put her hands in front of her chest and walked out as if she were stiff.

"I just came down to tell you that Mr. Johnson is very pleased with the way you are running the establishment," Mrs. Brown said. "You know, when a champion trains for a fight he must be able to relax in the evening and this place is quite quiet after supper."

"I'm glad he's pleased," I said.

When Mrs. Brown left, I sat at the desk and thought about what Gloria had said before we went to the warehouse. I called Chris. He wasn't home, but his mother answered and said that she would have him call me back.

I closed up the office and went out. The day was really warm. I just hadn't walked around for so long I forgot what it was like. Bubba's cousin was in the street with his crazy dog. The dog was trying to attack the street light.

I wandered over to the park and saw some kids playing basketball and I got into a game with them. They were a lot younger than me, and they kind of thought I would be a star because I was older than they were. I'm not bad, really, but I'm not a star. I played with them until it started getting dark. I thought some more about Gloria, how bad I felt that she had laughed at me.

When I got home, everybody was excited. My mother was crying and my father was all agitated.

"What happened at the warehouse yesterday?" he asked.

"The warehouse?"

"Dean told his parents that you and he and Gloria went

over to some warehouse and someone took a shot at you."

I told the whole story the best I could, and we had to go down to the precinct house. When we got there, Dean was already there. They had been over to the warehouse and found the guard that shot at us.

"Guard?"

"He claims that you and your friend were trying to steal from the warehouse," the policeman said.

"How about the stolen stuff on the third floor?" I asked.

"That's a legitimate warehouse," the policeman said. "As far as I know the only thing that happened is that you kids let your imaginations get the best of you. You almost got yourself killed in the process. The best thing I can say is that we can probably get the people who own the warehouse not to press charges, since you came in with your story."

I looked at Dean and he looked at me. We had to give the police a lot of information about what schools we went to and things like that. My mother was still crying.

"What I would suggest"—a heavyset detective named Jenkins was chewing on a cigar as he talked. Every time he said anything the cigar would bob up and down—"is that you kids go back to being what you can be—that is, a bunch of kids. Go on and have yourself some fun and stay out of places where you don't have any business being. If I hear anything more about either of you getting into trouble, I'm gonna make life rough on you. And don't expect your parents to get you out of trouble the next time. I don't care who comes down here crying and who don't. Now get out of here!"

I didn't know what had happened at the warehouse. I was

sure it was the one that Gloria and me had been to. Even in the dark it looked like the one.

When I got home my father started off with a lecture. I deserved it, every bit of it. And everything he said was true.

"You know, I came from a big family," he said. "You saw the place I lived in. It wasn't any better when I lived in it. My father couldn't any more support all of us than walk on water. So I say I'm just going to have one kid and take care of it. And now what? Now you go out and try to get yourself killed because some other kid gets himself in trouble. How come you didn't call Chris and tell him to go get his head shot off? I don't understand that!"

He went on asking me the same questions over and over. How was I going to tell him that I was beginning to think that maybe Chris did do it? Or that we needed the reward money to keep The Joint from going under?

He kept it up even after it didn't make any more sense to me any more. I could tell he was trying to get through to me, and I told him that I was sorry that I did it.

"Sorry?" His voice went up as if it was just changing or something. "Is that all you can say—that you're sorry?"

I sat quietly for a while, and so did he. He started to say something and then stopped. I realized that he didn't know what to say to me. He made a gesture with his hand, and that stopped as well. He didn't have any more answers to what I should have done or shouldn't have done than me. I don't know why, but when that thought came to me I felt really scared for a minute. It only lasted for a short time, but it was a different feeling. I felt very close to him after I stopped being scared. I knew I was sharing something with him. There were other things that I would have rather shared with him, but this was a very real thing. He seemed not to be as hard or as stiff as he usually seemed to me. He was okay, not as much as I thought, or as strong, but okay.

The next day I stayed around the house all day. Dean called and said he was sorry if I got into trouble because of him, but I said it was cool. I felt better that our parents knew about it. He asked me if I thought I could have made a mistake about the warehouse. I said yes, but I didn't really think so.

# CHAPTER
## 17

I DON'T KNOW WHAT SHOOK ME UP THE MOST. WHAT HAPpened in the warehouse was bad, but what happened later, going to the police station and everything, was nearly as bad. I got up early the next day and went to the library, just to be away from things for a while, and then I went to the movies. Gloria called that evening, but I told my mother I wasn't feeling well when she told me who it was, and that I would call her later. I didn't, of course.

The street fair was coming up, and I wanted to go to see what was going on at The Joint, but I didn't. I stayed in the house the next day, too. It rained most of the day, and I just hung around and watched some of the silly daytime quiz shows on television. When the doorbell rang, I thought it might be my mother. She was working that day, and I thought maybe she was home early. She hadn't been feeling too well lately, and sometimes she would come home in the middle of the day. It wasn't my mother. It was Gloria.

"Hi." She was standing there in the doorway with this big grin on her face.

"Hi," I answered.

"Can I come in?"

I moved away from the door and she came in. I went over and sat at the kitchen table. She came over to the sink and leaned against it.

"You know"—she had her head down and had stopped grinning—"I'm really sorry about the other night."

"Forget it," I said. "I did."

"I don't want to forget it," she said. She looked up at me and smiled again. Not smiled, but grinned.

"I don't see what's so funny," I said.

"That's just it," she said. "Nothing's funny. You said . . . you know . . . what you said, and I just got kind of embarrassed and I laughed. Even now, when I talk about it, I really feel embarrassed."

"So don't talk about it."

"I want to talk about it."

"Why, if you find it so embarrassing?" I pushed the salt shaker behind the sugar bowl with one finger and then brought it around the other side.

"I was embarrassed because of the way I felt when you said it, I guess," she said. "That and because I felt so good inside and so silly at the same time. I didn't know what to say or what to do. When you left I cried. I really did. I didn't even want to think about how I felt about you before. And then you said what you said . . . that you loved me . . . and it all came out, or up, or someplace. I don't know, I was just so glad that you said it. What I wanted to say to you then—or after you had left, really—was that I felt the same way about you. You know what I mean? I love you, too."

Now it was my time to feel stupid. I didn't say anything at all. Instead I pushed the salt shaker back around the sugar bowl. Only this time I pushed it the other way. I looked at Gloria and she was still standing there, leaning against the sink, fooling around with her fingers. I had the feeling she was waiting for me to say something cool. I remembered in a movie once when this girl was walking with a guy on a beach and she turned to him and said something like, "David, I love you very much." And there was this music playing in the background and he took her in his arms and said something about her meaning the whole world to him, and then they kissed and the movie ended as they walked along the beach. There wasn't any music playing, but I had to say something.

"Thanks, I needed that."

Gloria smiled again, and we didn't say anything for a while, and then she asked me if I wanted to go over to The Joint to see what was going on. It seemed like a good idea and I said okay.

"Before we go over," she said, "you want to kiss or anything?"

So I kissed Gloria Wiggens. I haven't kissed many girls, but I have to admit kissing Gloria wasn't the worst way to spend a little time.

When we got back to The Joint we found out that Mr. Hyatt was out of the hospital. He had lost a lot of weight and didn't look good at all. We all went up and said hello to him, and he said he appreciated us keeping his place for him and he'd have the rent straightened out as soon as he could. Then we had a meeting, and we decided at the meeting that we weren't going to get involved with the Chris caper any more. It was just too dangerous. We didn't know anything more than we had at first, and we—at least Dean and me— almost got ourselves shot. Bad news. We didn't even feel bad about it at this point. I said that I would tell Chris and that he would probably understand. We all vowed to still be his friend, though. We'd have to manage without the reward money.

It's funny about our block. Everybody does their own thing, so to speak, and leaves everybody else alone. But once when we had a street clean-up campaign everybody came and pitched in. Now when we were going to have the street fair everybody wanted to help. Some people volunteered to make free food, some helped with the decorations, some wanted to play instruments. I got the feeling after a while that there was going to be so much free stuff going on that we would end up not making any more money than we did at the rent party.

Bubba had one of his rare good ideas. He said that we should have our own little things. He got a scale and said that he would guess people's weight, and Gloria and her mother made chocolate candy which they wrapped up in tin foil to make them look like chocolate kisses. Tina and Johnnie Mae got some of their friends to hook up a loudspeaker and brought all of their records. There was some argument over whether we would have Puerto Rican records, West Indian records, disco, or just plain soul records. A Polish lady—the only white woman living on the block—wanted at least one polka and brought her own record. She said it came from the old country, but it had a Sears label on it. Somebody pointed that out to her, and she said that she had bought it in Union City, New Jersey. I guess that was as close to the old country as she had ever been.

I got my father involved in the street fair. No lie. I just asked him if he would give us a hand. At first he didn't say anything, and then he said okay, he would. And what he did was to go around and keep people moving. I didn't think that was very important at first, but I saw after a while that it was.

The most popular thing at first was Bubba's weight-guessing thing. He had a jar, one of those big jars, and you put a dime in the jar and he would guess your weight. If he didn't guess your weight to within five pounds he would give you your dime back. Now that sounded pretty silly, and it would have been except for the fact that all the guys were trying to get the girls to step on the scale and they didn't want to. Then some of the guys started betting among themselves who was the heaviest and things like that and they were all putting dimes into Bubba's jar and weighing themselves and trying to get the women to get on the scales. It was pretty funny, really.

When Tina and Johnnie Mae got the music going, the whole block was jumping. People were dancing in the street, on the sidewalk, everywhere. There were a lot of people from other blocks, but it didn't make any difference. Everyone was having a good time. Mr. Pender came with Mrs. Pender. I didn't even know there *was* a Mrs. Pender. She was in a wheelchair. He told Gloria that she had cerebral palsy, and that he spent as much time with her as possible. She had been all right until she reached forty, he said, and then they had been in an auto accident and she had gotten cerebral palsy as a result.

My mother had helped one of the ladies bake some cakes, and they were selling cakes and little tarts. Askia Ben Kenobi's lady, Miss Selassie, as he called her, was telling people's fortunes by writing their names on a piece of paper, burning the paper, and reading the ashes. She was as spooky as he was.

Things were working out just fine until Gloria got into a fight. There was a guy on the block named Luke who everybody used to call Homeboy. Wherever you said you were from, Homeboy would say that he used to live there. He was married to a girl who wasn't too pretty. In fact, Bubba said she looked like she had plastic surgery on her face and the surgeon didn't have anything but used parts when he did the job.

So Homeboy came up and asked Glória how much her kisses went for, and she said fifty-five cents apiece, two for a dollar.

"They're really good," Gloria said. And she held one out for him. Homeboy took a look at the candy kisses and said that he didn't mean anything wrapped up in silver paper. He wanted a real kiss.

Now Gloria had been going through this all the time, and

she didn't really mind because after people finished kidding around they usually bought one of her candy kisses.

"Now what am I going to do with these things?" Homeboy said. "What I need is the real thing."

"Well, what you need is one thing and what you can buy here is another thing."

Homeboy walked off in a huff, and Gloria started talking to Jeannie about this and that. The whole thing might have ended right there if it hadn't been for Homeboy running into Mr. Darden. Darden had started his still back up and was running what he called an upside-down beauty parlor.

"You goes to the regular beauty parlor," he said with a big smile on his face, "to get your hair curled. You come here to get your toes curled."

Homeboy bought some of Petey Darden's basement booze, mixed it with some Coca-Cola, and carried it around in a brown paper bag as he nipped on it. After he had nipped his way through most of the bag, he stumbled back over to where Gloria was trying to sell the last couple of kisses. Not only was he half bombed, but the booze had messed up his throat so bad he could hardly talk. He was just wheezing his words out. Gloria couldn't hear him when he asked her a question and kind of leaned over, and she turned her cheek.

Homeboy wasn't having any cheek turning. He turned Gloria's face back around and gave her a kiss. It must have been kind of a powerful kiss, or perhaps the booze on his breath put her under for a while because she didn't move. She just looked at him.

"Knew that would get you," Homeboy said. Then he

grabbed her and half pulled her out of the booth, kissing her like they used to in the movies back when kissing was a big thing. Gloria tried to get loose and the more she tried the harder Homeboy was holding her. A few people saw the whole thing—the kissing part at least—but they weren't sure what was going on. They could have been fooling around—it would have been some heavy fooling around, but it could have been. Finally Gloria got one hand free and punched Homeboy just above his left ear. Homeboy staggered back and then he started circling Gloria as if he was going to fight her. Some of the other guys started to go in and break it up, but it was too late. Gloria hit Homeboy on the jaw and knocked him down. Homeboy got up again and Gloria knocked him down again. He got up again and she hit him and he fell against a wall.

It was funny at first, the way Gloria had hit Homeboy and knocked him down. But then everybody saw that it wasn't just because Homeboy had been drinking. Gloria could just fight better than Homeboy! Homeboy got serious, but that didn't help anything. Gloria went upside his head so many times he must have thought her fists were part of a permanent hangover he had grown in his ear—a noisy part that hurt a lot.

We got the fight broken up and some guys helped Homeboy down the street toward where he lived. He was saying that if he ever caught Gloria alone he would punch her out.

"If you ever catch her alone you'd better look cross-eyed and hope she don't recognize your ugly butt!" Tina yelled at Homeboy. Then there was another fight up the street when two older guys had a foot race and one slipped and fell in some dog leavings. The guy who fell was mad, of course, and the other guy was just laughing. The streets were clean, but some dogs had wandered into the street fair and did their thing.

With the second fight people started drifting away. But then Tina got the microphone and called everybody back to the street.

"Everybody come over here for just one more minute!" Her voice echoed off the buildings as she talked through the loudspeaker. "Come on, you've had a nice time today, you can spare a minute!"

So everybody started gathering around the stoop she was standing on. And when they did, she called me, Gloria, Bubba, Dean, Omar, and anybody else she saw under nineteen and said we were the organizers of the party and to give us a big hand.

"Now we got these booths and things from the city and they're going to come by and pick them up," she said. "But they're not going to clean up the mess we made. We got two ways of doing that. Everybody can just clean in front of your own place, or we can all pitch in a dollar or fifty cents, whatever you got, and give it to these young people and they will do the cleaning!"

That really sounded like a good idea. And most people didn't want to clean the streets so they took up a big collection and five of us got brooms and stuff to start cleaning the street. We made extra money, so that was a good idea, right? Wrong!

Cleaning a street after a block party is about the hardest thing in the world. We started at one corner and started sweeping everything into the street. We figured we could sweep everything into the street and then the sidewalks would be clean and we could just go down the street and pick up the garbage. Good idea, right? Wrong again! Since the party was over, the police took down the barricades and started letting traffic through again, so when we had a big pile of garbage in the middle of the street a few cars spread half of it back across the width of the street. We started picking up a lot of the stuff and putting it into garbage cans and plastic bags. Hours. That's what it took. We didn't have the really big brooms that the sanitation department did or those garbage cans on wheels. Just bending down picking up everything was brutal.

We started off, me, Dean, Bubba, and Omar, laughing and joking and working as fast as we could. We lost Gloria right away because Mr. Pender came and took her away so they could figure out the money.

"How much you figure we made?" Bubba asked.

"About three hundred dollars," I said, really thinking it was a lot more than that.

"I bet it was a lot more than that," Bubba said.

"How we gonna split the money?" Omar asked.

"What do you mean?"

"Well, Tina said that all the kids in the block were responsible for the party, so I figure everybody should get a share," Omar said.

"Only the sponsors of the street party get the money," I said. "Why should you get anything? You didn't help do anything."

"I'm helping clean up," Omar said.

"Then you get part of the clean-up money they collected," Bubba said.

Omar said if that was all he was going to get, then we could forget it, and he dropped his broom and went home. He wasn't that anxious about working anyway. Neither were we, but we were stuck.

The street fair had started at five and ended at eight. We began cleaning about nine o'clock, and at eleven-thirty we were just getting finished. Two and a half hours of back-breaking work. When we got the last little bit cleaned up, a car came through and a girl who was riding in the back of it threw out some wrappers from Kentucky Fried Chicken and some chicken bones as the car sped past. One of the funniest things I ever saw in my life, and then it wasn't funny until the next day, was Dean standing in the middle of the street trying to hit a car a block and a half down the street with a chicken bone. You don't know what it means to have some-body dump garbage on your street until you're the one who has to clean it up.

"And you know what else makes me mad?" Bubba said. "Everybody is going to come out tomorrow and not even notice that the street is clean."

"Right," I said, "but they would notice if it was dirty."

We put all the cleaning stuff in the office at The Joint, and Bubba left. Me and Dean started to leave and made it to the stoop before we had to sit down again, we were just that tired. Dean was so tired he was getting whiny, like a little kid.

"Hey, bloods, what's happening?" It was Kelly Smith, Pat's older brother. They were a cousin to someone in Earth,

Wind & Fire, and Kelly had tried out with the Cleveland Cavaliers. He was about six six and had a way of leaning over you when he talked. Which wouldn't have been so bad if he had heard of Scope.

"Hey, Kelly, how's it going?"

"All right, all right," he said. "I got the weight and I'm definitely carrying the freight."

He put his hand up and we stuck out our palms and he gave us five. That was another thing about Kelly. He was always giving somebody five. By the time you finished talking to him, your fingers were swollen.

"Were you at the party?"

"I don't miss nothing dynamite," Kelly said, "and this was dynamite and out of sight! It helped my day and made the night!"

Slap. Slap.

"It was a lot of work," Dean said.

"I think you cats should give a party like this every week," Kelly said. "Check it out! This could be the party capital of the world. You get all the downtown freaks coming up here to disco to the outdoor sound, and boogying with the people."

Slap. Slap.

"Too much work," Dean said, trying to rub some life back into his legs. "It took us almost three hours to get the street clean."

"Yeah, and then some woman threw a box of Kentucky Fried Chicken and some chicken bones out the window of her car."

"You can run the money end, see," Kelly said, "and have

your old lady run the social part, dig it? You got an old lady?"

"Yeah," I said.

"What's her name?"

"Gloria." I held my breath when I said that. I was glad nobody else was around, especially Gloria, when I said that she was my old lady.

"No lie? You really got an old lady named Gloria?"

"Uh-huh."

"I used to have an old lady named Gloria," Kelly said.

Slap. Slap.

"Oh, yeah?"

"Yeah, everybody thought she was ugly, but she wasn't. She was handicapped. I could see people thinking she was ugly because the first time I seen her I thought she was ugly, too. But she was just handicapped. She was born with her lips on wrong. The top lip was where the bottom lip was supposed to be and the bottom lip was stuck up on top. That made her look funny."

"I can understand it," I said.

"She talked funny, too," Kelly said.

"I can understand that, too," I said.

"But you could tell she wasn't ugly or nothing," Kelly went on, "because she had a little mustache and that was in the right place, and if you could kinda imagine her bottom lip up on top she was kinda cute."

"Sometimes you have to use your imagination a little," I said.

"Right on."

Slap. Slap.

"I wish I could have used my imagination to get the street clean," I said. "We worked like dogs getting all that paper and stuff up."

"Hey, look." Kelly was hovering over us and it was pretty rough. It was like something had died in his mouth. "You can hire some flunkies to do that kind of work, and you and your man here can be the man-o, man-o-gerial staff. Can you dig it?"

Slap. Slap.

"Then after a while you become famous and everybody will flock to the place. When it rains you hold it indoors, see?"

"We don't have a place to hold it indoors," Dean said. "And the booths and loudspeaker and stuff don't belong to us either. We got the booths and the loudspeaker from the park people."

"The Department of Parks," I said.

"Don't be mean, baby," Kelly said, exhaling. "You can hold the thing in your place. It'll be like a ongoing rent party. A different kind of music in every pad. I can get you some boss stereo equipment at half price, and I know a cat who can get a lot of downtown chicks to come. That's all you really need, man, the chicks. If you get some foxes all you got to do is stand around and hum, the foxes will take care of everything else!"

Slap. Slap.

"Well, we'll think about it," I said. My mind was jumping around to so many places I couldn't even think straight. I wondered if Dean had picked up on the bit about the stereo stuff.

"You know what we should do," Dean said, "check out the prices of everything we would need. We'd have to paint all the places—that would cost money—probably do some decorating, figure out how much the stereo stuff would cost, and figure out how we could get cheap food—"

"Man, the idea can't lose!" Kelly interrupted. "Paint don't cost nothing much, and you don't need to decorate the place all up. You just got to give it a cool name. I used to know a place that some cats bought to make into a bar. This cat's aunt went to the hospital, and everybody thought she was going to die and leave this dude a piece of change. So they went out and bought a place that wasn't much more than a cellar. They figured as soon as the cat's aunt kicked off they'd get the money and decorate the place up. But she was one of them mean old West Indian chicks what refused to kick off. So they opened the place and called it The Cellar and it made a fortune. You can call this place something cool and you won't have no decorating to do, man."

"Stratford Arms Disco."

"Right on! If they can have a singer called Meat Loaf, you can have a disco called Stratford Arms!" Kelly said. "And I can take you over to a cat got a stereo store near La Marqueta, and he'll give you stereo stuff at a boss price."

We told him we would think about it, and Dean said we could go look at the stuff Saturday, and Kelly said okay. Then he went on talking about how much money we could make and stuff like that until I couldn't keep my eyes open any more. The thing was that a lot of the stuff he was saying seemed to make sense. But the thing that was on my mind most was the stereo stuff.

"What do you think?" I asked Dean when Kelly left.

"I think we should forget about this whole thing," Dean said.

"I guess so," I answered. "What do you think?"

"You already asked me that."

"Oh."

"Probably wouldn't do any harm just looking, though," he said.

"I guess not," I answered.

I said good-bye to Dean at his place and started across to my place when I heard him call to me. I turned and he was just crossing the street.

"Look," he said, "if you can convince yourself that this is really stupid and that we shouldn't do it, call me right away and work on me, okay?"

172

# CHAPTER 18

MY FATHER SAYS I SLEEP THE SLEEP OF THE DEAD. NOTHING wakes me. Once my parents had gone out and I had put the chain on the door and fell asleep, and they banged on the door, called on the telephone, and even went to Mrs. Lucas's house next door and banged on the wall—nothing. Finally my father had to come in through the fire-escape window. My mother thought I had either been drugged or had died in my sleep. They woke me up finally after shaking me for a minute. What can I tell you?—that's the way I sleep. After I got home from cleaning up the street and the party and so forth, I said good night to my parents and went in to bed. Then I had this weird dream.

I dreamed that I was playing third base for Cincinnati.

They had hired me to replace some star that had gone to another team. I was hitting about .400 and hadn't made an error. The season was almost over and two of our pitchers had been hurt in an auto accident. We just managed to win the pennant and then the league playoffs, mostly due to my hitting, and now we were in the series. Another of our pitchers was hurt—he pulled a tendon in his right leg and couldn't throw. The two pitchers we had had pitched all the games. They were exhausted. There was no way they could pitch the last game of the series. This was it—do or die. The manager came to me.

"Paul," he said, "you know what you have to do."

I knew. He handed me the ball and I took the mound. I pitched the first four innings without giving up a hit. In the top of the fifth I shook off one sign from the catcher and then another. He came out to the mound and started in this long argument about he knew what pitching was all about, that I was just a third baseman and I'd better wake up to that fact.

"Wake up, kid," he said. He was shaking me by the shoulder.

"No, I don't want to wake up," I said, "I can pitch as well as anybody in this league!"

"Wake up, Paul, wake up!"

I opened my eyes, and it was my father. I looked around for the rest of the team and they weren't there.

"Paul, are you awake?"

"Yeah," I answered through the fog, "I guess so."

"There's a phone call for you," he said. "That Mrs. Brown from the building."

"What time is it?"

"Two-thirty."

"In the morning?"

"In dreams begin responsibilities."

I stumbled through the dining room to where the phone sat on the hutch. I answered it and listened while Mrs. Brown told me, in tears, that Jack Johnson had just died. She asked me would I come over to help her with the arrangements. I asked could it wait until morning, and she said she thought I had better come right over.

"Is anything wrong?" My mother was tying the belt of her housecoat. "It's so early in the morning. . . ."

"Jack Johnson just died again," I said.

"Again?" My mother looked at my father.

"There's this woman, Mrs. Brown," I said. "She thinks she lives with Jack Johnson, and about once a month she tells us that he died. But after a while he comes back to life again, or she forgets that he was supposed to have died, or something."

"What are you going to do?" my mother asked. "You can't have her calling you at all hours in the morning."

What I wanted to do was to go back to bed. But Mrs. Brown had been crying. I decided that Jack Johnson would probably be alive in the morning, though, and went back to bed. Then I thought about Mrs. Brown waiting for me or someone to come over, and I got up again. I told my parents that I would go over and talk to her and would probably be right back.

I had only been in Mrs. Brown's apartment once or twice. It was full of smells. She had alcohol and this mentholated

175

cream that she used to put on herself to "ward away colds and fevers" and cocoa butter which she put on her face. When I got there she was still crying a little and said that Mr. Johnson was in the next room.

That was a little scary. Suppose there *was* somebody in the next room? Dead. I went to the door holding my breath and looked in. There was a big brass bed in the middle of the floor. The whole room looked like something from the olden days. There were pictures of Jack Johnson around the room. Some of them were in his boxing trunks and some in street clothes. What I didn't see, thank goodness, was any real people laying around dead.

I sat with Mrs. Brown for the rest of the night. She fell asleep, and I did, too. I woke first and she was sitting in the chair near the window. It was just daylight. I could hear the sound of a radio coming from one of the floors below us. Then I heard a swishing noise and the sound of a window opening slowly.

"I hear that window going up!" Mr. Darden. "I'm watching, too!"

Mr. Darden used to sweep the alleyway between The Joint and the next building. And every time he would sweep someone would throw down a bag of water or an empty milk container at him. So what he would do would be to stand against the side of the building and make sweeping noises with the broom and watch to see what window opened. I guess he figured if he could see who was doing it they wouldn't have the nerve to do it. Anyway, he started making more sweeping noises and kept that up until he figured he was safe. Then he started sweeping. I heard the bag of water hit, and I heard Mr. Darden start swearing. He knew some swear words I had never even heard before.

It was kind of funny, really—Mr. Darden yelling up at whoever it was that threw the bag of water at him. It also woke up Mrs. Brown. She was a little startled to see me there, and said how nice it was of me to visit.

"Mr. Johnson is sleeping late today," she said. "But if you come a little later, after he's done his roadwork, we can all have breakfast together."

I told her I'd like that and left. I wondered what the world looked like from her eyes, and what part of it she was living now and what part of it she was just living in memory.

I went home and told my parents what had happened, and they said how sorry they felt for Mrs. Brown, which was more or less what I expected them to say. I tried to get some sleep but I couldn't so I went over to The Joint again.

Now, Gloria was there and I had already told Gloria how I felt about her and everything. So there we were in the office at The Joint, talking about the party and the fight and everything, except I was thinking about how I had kissed her. The thing was, when I was outside with Gloria I didn't particularly want anybody to know how I felt about her, but when I was alone with her it was different. Not that I wanted anybody else to know how I felt, but I liked saying that I cared for her, even though it was a little embarrassing. Also, I liked kissing her. I wanted to get the conversation around to that before Mr. Pender came over. He was supposed to come over and tell us how we did from the party. Gloria said that they had done some figuring and it looked really good.

"I think we made enough money to keep us going until after school starts," Gloria said.

"Hey, look," I said—my usual cool beginning—"you want to go out or anything?"

"Go out where?" she said. "Mr. Pender's going to be here any minute."

"I mean on a date or something?"

"With you?"

There she went smiling again. That really ticked me off, because her smile (and I had really thought about this) was just about a laugh for most people. And as soon as I saw her smile I didn't want to talk about it any more. She got up from the desk where she always sat when we were in the office and came up to where I was standing next to the linen closet. Then she gave me a little kiss just as the door opened. It was Tina Robinson.

"You people at it again?" she said. "At least you got yourselves out of the bathroom."

That was the end of that. But that was good, because I really had to take Gloria in small doses. Not that I didn't like her or anything, because I was crazy about her, but I felt so different when I was around her I was almost a different person. Even more so when we were alone.

When Tina left (she just dropped in to say hello) I told Gloria about what had happened with Kelly and how me and Dean were thinking about going over to the place he said there were stereos. She was about to say something when Mr. Pender came in.

According to Mr. Pender, we had done well with the street fair but not as well as Bubba and me had thought.

After we had paid all our bills we had made a net profit of four hundred and two dollars. Then Mr. Pender said we should keep one hundred and fifty dollars aside in case we come up with some bills from the fair that we didn't know about

"And our bills only come up to two hundred and eight dollars," Mr. Pender said. "That includes payment to the accountant of some fifty dollars . . ."

He hesitated and looked at Gloria and me.

"Good!" I said, and Gloria echoed my feelings. I was glad that Mr. Pender was finally getting paid something, at least.

We talked some more about the party and about the house, and then we got around to talking to Mr. Pender about the Chris caper again. We told him what had happened with the warehouse bit and then again with Kelly Smith. I also told him what had happened with my father, about how upset he had been.

"Well, I can see that," Mr. Pender said. "Sometimes you want to avoid any kind of risks. But there has to be a balance somewhere. An Englishman—I believe his name was Housman—once wrote a poem that went something like this:

> When I was one-and-twenty
> I heard a wise man say,
> 'Give crowns and pounds and guineas
> But not your heart away;'

"It was probably the worst advice I had ever heard in my entire life," Pender went on. "I don't mean that you should do anything that's just out-and-out foolish, but there are certain little chances that one confronts in life that seem to give meaning to the whole. Do you know what I mean?"

"No."

That seemed to disappoint Mr. Pender a bit—that we didn't know what he was talking about. But he did seem to be in favor of checking out our new lead.

"Although it probably won't work," he said. "The stolen items, to the best of my knowledge, were all fairly standard equipment. We'd have to go around checking identification numbers of the stuff, which might very well be in a back room or somehow inaccessible unless we were willing to actually buy it. And that, of course, seeing how limited our funds already are, would hardly be worth the risk."

"That's for sure," Gloria agreed.

We talked for a while longer, but my mind was already racing ahead. I could hardly wait for Mr. Pender to finish telling us about our new financial status, which was predictably gloomy, and leave. I told Gloria that I had to see Dean about a basketball tournament we were thinking of entering. She said okay, but I felt she was a little disappointed that I didn't get back to talking about taking her out. There would be time for that later, I thought.

When I got to Dean's house, I found him sitting in the bathroom, sorting out his dirty socks, looking for a pair that wasn't too dirty to wear. I told him about my idea.

"You got to be crazy, man," he said, sniffing a pair of tubes. "You can't use the money we got from the street fair to buy the stuff. Suppose it's not the stuff?"

"I know it's the stuff," I said. "I just know it. I can feel it in my bones."

"What did Gloria say?"

"I didn't tell her."

" 'Cause you know she wouldn't go for it," he said. "We go over and buy that stuff and it's not the right stuff we're just going to be out the money and right back where we started from."

"What's the matter?" I asked. "You afraid?"

"What's today?"

"What's today?" I repeated his question. "Friday. Why?"

"Because Friday isn't one of my stupid days," he said. "But check me out on Wednesday or Saturday—those are my stupid days."

"Look, I know it's going to work. It's a bold move, I know, but we're bold dudes!"

"And you're going to take all the heat if we just blow the money?"

"All the heat," I said.

"And tell Gloria that it was all your idea?"

"Yeah, I guess so."

"You *guess* so?"

"I'll tell her it was all my idea."

"You got a plan?" he asked, pulling on a pair of slightly stiff socks.

"I got a plan."

# CHAPTER 19

IT WAS EASIER GETTING BUBBA INVOLVED THAN IT WAS Dean. Bubba was basically a more straightforward person than Dean was. With Dean you had to cajole and badger and argue with him until two things happened—one, he was convinced, and, secondly, he was convinced more than he was scared. With Bubba you could take a more direct approach, usually a bribe. We offered Bubba a pizza if he would go along without telling Gloria until it was over. We had to involve Bubba because Kelly didn't know him. He knew Dean.

We got the money from the office where we had it locked in a drawer. Dean was to stay in the office and tell Gloria or Mr. Pender that I had taken the money home for safekeeping, if they asked. He was also there to act as our backup man. If I called and asked to speak to Charlie, he would know we were in trouble.

Bubba was dressed in his Sunday suit and was wearing shades. That was my idea so that he looked a little like an underworld guy. It was his idea to carry a handkerchief and keep wiping his neck with it. He had seen that on the Late Show. I think he looked okay, but Kelly didn't take to him at all.

"Who is this cat?" he asked.

"He's the bag man," I said, trying to act cool.

"The *what*?" Kelly asked.

"Our bag man," I said, wondering if the people working on the SALT talks knew about Kelly's breath. "He carries anything that's a little ... you know ..."

"What you mean, man?" Kelly looked Bubba over.

"I mean"—I lowered my voice to a whisper and looked around—"that when we do anything a little ... you know ..."

"No lie?" Kelly looked at me.

"No lie," I answered.

"He don't look the type to me," Kelly said.

"Now you know why we use him."

"Hey, I can dig it," he said, nodding. "All riiight!"

We went over to where Bubba was standing with his briefcase in his hand. Bubba didn't say anything to Kelly when Kelly spoke to him, just grunted a little and wiped his neck with his handkerchief. We got the crosstown bus and then walked half a block until we reached the small store. It was crowded with furniture and signs. Sometimes you couldn't even see the furniture for the signs. The signs read "3 rooms of furniture, $295"—or "No money down, 2 years to pay"—things like that. A short stocky guy wearing a suit and a small cap came up to us.

"Hey, Kelly, what's happening," he said, shaking Kelly's hand but looking right at me and Bubba. "How's it going, man?"

"It's going okay, Tony," Kelly said. "Look, my friends here are interested in getting a good price on some stereo equipment. I told them you could give them a special price."

"Yeah, yeah." Tony looked me and Bubba over. "What kinds of things you looking for?"

"Some stereo equipment," I said, feeling kind of confident.

"Well, we got some nice stuff," he said. "About how much you want to spend?"

"It depends," Bubba said, "on how much we can get for our money."

"Well, why don't you take a look at this set?" Tony took us over to a stereo set that was made into a combination bar and fake fireplace. There was a price on the set. It was three hundred and sixty-seven dollars. There was another price, five hundred and ninety-nine dollars, that had a line through it, as if it had just been reduced. "This is a nice set, a lot of people are buying it."

"What's the price?" Bubba asked, looking at the price sign.

"It's right there," Tony said. "But you can pay on time if you don't have the money."

"We have the money," Bubba said, taking out a roll of

bills, "but the price isn't what we're looking for. We might have to buy two or three systems . . ."

"Well, you can buy as many systems as you want on credit," Tony said.

Kelly had walked away and was talking to one of the salesgirls. I didn't know what to say next. Bubba reached into the bar and turned on the set. It sounded pretty good. Then he turned it off and walked over to an amplifier. He turned that on and listened for a while.

"How many things can you plug into this?" he asked.

"What you got?" Tony asked. "This set can take a tape deck, a phonograph. How many things can you use at one time?"

Bubba grunted and wiped at his neck with the handkerchief. Then he started this little twitch with his mouth, as if something was jerking at his bottom lip. He was getting carried away with the whole bit.

"Look, you guys see anything you want, you let me know, okay?" Tony turned and walked over to where Kelly was standing looking at a turntable. He started talking to Kelly, but we could tell he was talking about us because he kept looking over his shoulder at us.

"Hey, Bubba, don't go overboard," I whispered.

Bubba grunted and wiped his neck with the handkerchief.

He turned on a few more sets, pretended like he was listening to them and then turned them off. Tony came back over and asked us if we saw anything we liked. He couldn't keep his eyes off Bubba, and Bubba was wiping faster and faster.

"I don't think we can"—Bubba wiped three times,

twitched his mouth twice, and then wiped again—"because your price isn't what we're looking for."

"That's the way it goes, my friends," Tony said, rubbing at his chin.

"Yeah," Bubba said, "and, like, later."

We started toward the door. Kelly caught up with us just before we got outside, and he pulled me aside.

"Look, man," Kelly said, "Tony thinks your friend is a dope fiend. He figures he just wants to case the place and come back and rip him off."

Kelly motioned for Tony to come over.

"Look, you want to do business with me it's okay," Tony said. "But I ain't looking for no trouble."

"He ain't no dope fiend," Kelly said, "he's just their bag man."

"What kind of bag he in?" Tony asked.

"I don't know," Kelly said. "Tell him, Paul."

"He's the *bag* man, dig it?" I whispered to Tony. "He carries the stuff when it's a little . . . you know . . ."

"Oh," Tony said, looking over at Bubba, who was still wiping and twitching, "he do?"

"Say, Mr. B.!" I called to Bubba, and he came over.

"You call him Mr. B.?" Tony asked.

"Never call him by his right name," I said under my breath as Bubba came over.

"What's up?" Bubba said, only now his voice was changing, too.

"Show him the bread," I said.

Bubba opened the briefcase where we had put the money. It looked like more than it was when you looked down at it.

186

Anyway, Bubba just gave Tony a quick look and then shut the bag again.

"Ain't no junkie got that kind of bread, baby," Kelly said, obviously impressed.

Tony was impressed, too. A moment later we were in the back room looking at boxes of stereo equipment. Tony said we could have anything we wanted at fifty dollars a box. In another minute we had selected six boxes.

"Get us a cab, man," Bubba said. He was beginning to sound a little like Marlon Brando in *The Godfather.*

I got the cab and we loaded all the boxes in the trunk and some in the front seat with the driver while me, Bubba, and Kelly sat in the back. Kelly whispered something into Bubba's ear, and Bubba opened the briefcase and took out a twenty-dollar bill and gave it to him. We dropped Kelly off near Morningside Avenue. It took us exactly forever to get back to The Joint and to unload the stuff in the cab. We took it all in the office and closed the door.

"You see how that cab driver looked at us?" Bubba said. "That guy was scared stiff!"

"You got all the stuff from that store?" Dean asked. "How much did you spend?"

Bubba opened the briefcase. We had twenty-three dollars left. I got this sinking feeling in the pit of my stomach. Dean held the money that was left in his hand, and it didn't look like very much. The original money that we had had from the street fair hadn't been much, but at least it was something.

"Let's get at those numbers," I said.

We dug out the list of serial numbers that Chris had given

us and began to check them against the numbers on the boxes. They didn't match. Not one number came even close to any of the boxes.

Checkout time. The sky had fallen. We just sat in the office without saying anything. Dean looked at the list again. He looked at the numbers on the boxes. He dropped the list on the desk.

When we heard Gloria's voice, talking to one of the Robinson sisters, we felt sick. She tried to get in and the door was locked and she knocked. I opened the door.

"Who died?" she asked.

"We thought—" I took a deep breath and started again. "I thought I had a good idea, but it didn't work out."

"What was the idea?" she asked, looking first at one face and then the other.

"I thought that if we bought the stuff from the store that Kelly said he had seen it in . . ."

"You mean what we were talking about before?" Gloria asked.

"Yeah."

She looked at the boxes and at the list of numbers on the table.

"How much is left?" she asked.

Dean pointed to the twenty-three dollars on the desk. Gloria looked at me and then counted the money. Then, as if she couldn't believe it, she counted it again. She didn't say anything else, just stood up and left the office.

# CHAPTER 20

WHEN I GOT HOME, MY FATHER WAS MAKING HAMBURGERS. My mother had gone somewhere shopping. He was in a good mood. He liked to cook. Even though he wasn't the best cook around, it always seemed to cheer him up when he made supper.

"How's it going?" he asked.

"Okay," I said, going past him to my room.

I fell across the bed and just lay there for a while. I tried to think of something, but I couldn't. I thought of taking back the stuff we had bought, but I knew it wouldn't work. I felt as if I were at the bottom of a deep pit that was getting deeper by the minute.

"Paul?" My father stood at the door.

"Yeah?"

"You want to talk about whatever's bothering you?"

"No." It came automatically, and he turned and left the room. I thought about it for a minute and then went into the kitchen where he was just turning off the burners.

"I assume you're not hungry," he said.

"Can I tell you about what happened?" I asked.

"Sure," he said, sitting down.

I told him the whole dismal story. He knew most of it, about how we had been trying to raise the money and everything, and about the reward. I just added the part about me still being involved in trying to find out who stole the stuff and how I blew the money. I halfway expected him to blow up, but he didn't. He didn't say anything, even after I had finished. When he didn't, I went back to my room. At least he didn't blow up.

My mother got home, and I listened to see if he would tell her, but he didn't. She knew something was up, but as usual she didn't push it. Later, when she was in the tub, he came into my room again.

"What do you mean, the numbers weren't even close?" he asked.

"What do *you* mean?" I asked.

"Were the first numbers different? Were there the same amount of numbers? What?" he asked.

"There were like five numbers on the list for each piece," I said, still not knowing what he was driving at, "and the boxes had about seven numbers and a few letters."

"Did you check the sets themselves," he asked, "or just the boxes?"

"You mean they might have changed the numbers on the boxes?"

"No, you might have checked the wrong numbers," he said. "You want to take another walk down to the office with me?"

Anything was better than just sitting there. He grabbed a few tools and we told my mother we'd be right back.

We got to the office and he looked at the list of numbers that Chris had given us and checked them against the boxes. Then we opened one of the boxes and we looked on the back of the set. The number wasn't the same as on the list but it was the same kind of number. That is, it had five digits and no letters, just the way the numbers on the list had. We started checking the other boxes. On the fifth one we struck gold. The numbers matched. The sixth one did, too. We had been right after all!

The night couldn't go fast enough. I called Gloria, Dean, and Bubba and told them what had happened. We agreed to meet at The Joint the first thing in the morning. Naturally, my father was there, too.

We were all really up, and when Tina and Johnnie Mae came in, it was my father who explained how we had found the stolen stuff. We were happy for about two or three minutes, until we called in a cop that was walking by.

"If it ain't happening right now, it's not in my jurisdiction," the heavy, puffy-faced policeman said. "What you got to do is to call the precinct."

A moment later my father was calling the precinct and was being told that we had already been warned about getting ourselves involved in police business.

"And how about this stolen merchandise?" asked my father.

He was told that a detective would be around in a day or two to question us about it. In a day or two the stuff could be gone, as it had been in the warehouse, we said. It was no use—in a day or two was the best he could do, he said.

"You want some action right now?" Tina asked. "Because if you do I can get this whole thing cleared up right away."

That we did.

"But let's not get into any danger," my father said.

"I got somebody that's going to keep us out of danger and get the police to moving their butts!"

Tina went upstairs, and we busied ourselves telling Dean and Bubba what had happened when they showed up. The next thing we heard was Tina coming down the stairs yelling at somebody.

"You better come on, turkey!" She was yelling at Askia Ben Kenobi! "You owe these kids something. You don't pay your rent, you done messed up their rent party—now you come on with us."

So the group of us locked up the office and marched over to the store that we had bought the equipment from. I was pretty nervous about the whole thing, but Tina wasn't. She told us all to stand outside and then she told Askia Ben Kenobi to stand in the doorway and not to let anybody in or out until she told him to. Then she stood in front of the door, cleared her throat, and started screaming!

"HELLLP! PO-O-O-O-O-LEEEESE! HELLLLLP! PO-O-O-O-O-LEEEEESE!"

Nobody could figure out what was going on. Tony came

out to see what was wrong, and Askia Ben Kenobi, robes flying, started jumping around in his karate poses. Tony backed off. Meanwhile Tina just kept screaming.

"HELLLLLP! PO-O-O-O-O-LEEEEESE!"

A crowd started gathering around.

"That Arab just stole her pocketbook!" one guy said, making up an instant story.

"I think the guy inside is trying to get his money from her and that A-rab is her boyfriend," another guy said.

By this time Tony, who thought the whole thing was pretty funny at first, had looked out and saw Bubba and me. He knew something was up. He grabbed a club that he kept behind the door and went after Ben Kenobi. No good. Ben knocked the club out of his hand with a flying kick. Then he started breaking up stuff in the store. He was going berserk. A squad car pulled up and two policemen got out. A second later another car came up and in minutes the street was filled with cops. Tina ran in and got Askia Ben Kenobi calmed down, and we went in and told the police the whole story. The police made Tony open the back room and they found all the stolen stuff.

"The detective told us that Tony didn't steal the stuff, after all," Mr. Pender told us at The Joint.

"I don't believe it!" my father said. "We found the equipment in his place."

"That's right," Chris said. "But he didn't steal it. Mr. Reynolds arranged for Willie Bobo to take part of the stuff over to Tony's place and keep part of it. He sold it to Tony for a cheap price and claimed all of it on his insurance. But when Willie got caught with his share there was a problem."

"Then when they arrested Chris, Willie was happy. He figured that since Chris was innocent they would both get off," Mr. Pender continued. "He wanted to drop charges, but the insurance company didn't let him. He felt bad about Chris getting arrested, but he knew the only way he could really clear Chris was to admit his own guilt. And Willie Bobo knew that as long as Chris was involved the chances of his going to jail were reduced. Except that Chris couldn't prove he was innocent."

"And everybody—well, a lot of us just assumed that he was guilty because he was involved," my father said.

"Exactly," continued Mr. Pender. "Except for Paul and his friends. Their concern, along with a little savvy from Paul's father, broke the case."

We were all happy for a while, but things didn't work out exactly the way we thought they would. Tony, the guy that bought the stuff from Mr. Reynolds, got a six months' suspended sentence. Willie Bobo and Mr. Reynolds we thought would go to jail for sure. It didn't turn out that way. What happened was that Willie Bobo stuck to the story that Chris was in on it even though everybody knew he wasn't. But Willie Bobo said that Mr. Reynolds had given Chris part of the money they had made from selling the stuff. It turned out that the money that Mr. Reynolds had given Chris wasn't really vacation money and, even worse, Chris knew it. It wasn't that Chris had stolen anything, but after Mr. Reynolds started giving him money, he had figured out that his boss was involved somehow. And he had taken the money. So in order not to get Chris involved they made a deal with Willie Bobo and Mr. Reynolds to accept suspended sentences.

When we found out about how Chris was involved, we didn't feel right taking the reward money, so we didn't. We thought we would just try to do more of the work ourselves and to get by the best we could. We thought we were having troubles with The Joint during the summer, but it was much worse in the winter. The fuel bills seemed to eat up every penny we earned and then some. Mr. Harley, the guy who had sold us the building in the first place, came around, and when he saw that we were keeping the building going, he got a friend of his to offer us another building on the same block for a few hundred dollars. We didn't have the money for it, but the Captain did, and he bought it and hired us to run it for him. That made things a little easier because the people in the other building paid their rents fairly regularly, and having two buildings actually helped because we began to get discounts on some things because we bought a lot. Mr. Pender says that we'll have The Joint making a profit, if everything works out and we have just a little luck, in about two years.

Petey Darden and his wife moved out, and Askia Ben Kenobi moved down into the basement. Now he takes care of the maintenance and things, and he gives karate lessons down there, too. You get used to the karate yells and things after a while, and even the people who hate the noise say that they haven't been bothered much by burglaries lately. One of the things that got Askia Ben Kenobi quieted down was that he got a little sweet on Tina Robinson. She even got him to wearing regular clothes most of the time. Every now and then he greases himself up, though, and runs around in one of his costumes.

When our first winter was almost over and I had just managed to pay what I hoped to be the last big fuel bill for the year, my father asked me if I had the chance to buy the building again, knowing what it would mean, if I still would. I said I didn't know, but I would think about it and let him know. We talk a lot more now, me and my father. He's still my father, but I think I'm coming from a slightly different place than I was before I got involved with The Joint.

I had wanted the fun of owning a place, but I hadn't wanted the responsibility. But even that wasn't as important as having the responsibility and being faced with the idea of wanting to give it up. I learned a lot from The Joint about people, how they lived and all, which was basically cool. I learned to accept the idea that answers were a lot easier to come by when you stood across the street from the problem. What was a lot harder to accept was that there weren't good answers to every problem, and when there weren't good answers you had to make do the best you could. That was hard sometimes, really hard, to accept.

Mostly the whole experience was an up kind of thing, though. Because we had made it work, even though it wasn't always rewarding. And then we had gotten close to a lot of people in the bargain. And it was still a lot of fun sometimes.

Me and Gloria were talking about it the other day in the office, and she felt pretty much the same way. We must have talked longer than we thought and it was almost midnight when Tina Robinson knocked on the door to the office.

"What are you people doing in here this time of night?"

Tina asked. She had her hands on her hips and a big smile on her face.

"Tina, we weren't doing anything," Gloria said.

"Confess, Paul!" Tina put her nose right up to mine and I had to smile.

"Tina—" I started, but she was already laughing and backing out the door.

"Love'll make you do some strange things," she said. "Some *strange* things."

I guess it will. She was heading toward the basement and Askia Ben Kenobi.

I walked Gloria home and then went home myself. When I got home, there was a note in my room that someone had called and said that they had dropped their keys down the drain in the kitchen sink. I didn't even wonder how anybody could do something like that any more. I just picked up a pencil and put "Bubba's turn" down on the bottom.